APPLAUSE FOR

MURDER IN THE TITLE

SIMON BRETT,
And His
Charles Paris Mysteries

Also by Simon Brett

Cast, in Order of Disappearance
Star Trap*
Murder Unprompted*
Situation Tragedy*
So Much Blood
A Comedian Dies*
The Dead Side of the Mike*
An Amateur Corpse*
A Series of Murders*

*Published by
WARNER BOOKS

MURDER IN THE TITLE

A CHARLES PARIS MYSTERY
SIMON BRETT

WARNER BOOKS

A Time Warner Company

WARNER BOOKS EDITION

Copyright © 1983 by Simon Brett

This Warner Books Edition is published by arrangement with
Charles Scribner's Sons, an imprint of Macmillan Publishing
Company, 866 Third Avenue, New York, NY 10022.

Cover illustration by John Martinez

Warner Books, Inc.
666 Fifth Avenue
New York, N.Y. 10103

 A Time Warner Company

Printed in the United States of America

First Warner Books Printing: November, 1990

10 9 8 7 6 5 4 3 2 1

To Little Fat Jack

ACT ONE

CHAPTER
ONE

SUNLIGHT, FILTERED THROUGH the stained glass armorial bearings of the De Meaux family, splashed bloodstains on the painted flooring. The maid, Wilhelmina, pert in her black and white uniform, entered through the heavy oak door to answer the telephone's insistent summons.

"Good afternoon, Wrothley Grange," she intoned, economically providing both temporal and spatial information for those unable to afford programs.

"No, I'm afraid Sir Reginald De Meaux is not available at the moment. When he's working on his collection of dueling swords in the study he does not like to be disturbed," she continued, thoughtfully revealing the name and a little of the character of her employer, as well as planting a useful murder weapon.

"I'm sorry, Mr. Laurence, the butler, has just had to pop down to the village," she apologized, raising comforting expectations that, when Something was Done, there would be at least one obvious suspect who might have Done It.

"No, I'm afraid Lady Hilda is in the rose garden and Master James is playing tennis with Miss Kershaw," she responded, filling out the cast list a little.

"No. Professor Weintraub has gone for a walk with Miss

Laycock-Manderley and Colonel Fripp," she continued, mopping up most of the rest of the cast.

"What, me?" Coy giggle. "Oh, sir, you don't want to know my name. Well, it's Wilhelmina," she confessed readily, completing the dramatis personae (except for the policeman in Act Three).

"Oh yes, certainly sir, I'll take a message. Just let me get a pencil and paper."

This she did, and stood with the one poised over the other. "Right, I'm ready. Yes, and the message is . . . ? What? Did you say . . . 'Murder'?"

She looked at the receiver with eight-years-at-stage-school's worth of amazement.

"Who's there? Who's there?" she demanded, jiggling the buttons of the telephone.

She replaced the receiver and looked out front. "Well, I declare," she said, momentarily perplexed.

But her confusion was short-lived. "Must have been a crank," she concluded with an easily satisfied shrug, and went over to the mantelpiece, her feather duster poised, to draw attention to another potential murder weapon, a heavy brass candlestick.

With her back thus conveniently to the French windows, she did not perceive the entrance of James De Meaux, dressed, for reasons of plot, in dazzling tennis whites and, for reasons of vanity, in a lot of body make-up. She did not see him deposit his racket on a leather armchair, nor apparently was she aware of his approach behind her until his arms were chastely round her waist.

"Oh, Mr. James," she protested, fluttering her feather duster without much conviction in order to evade his grasp.

"Come on, Willy. One little kiss," James demanded roguishly.

"No, James, not here. Someone might come in. I must go." She made for the door, but was prevented from reaching it.

"You weren't so coy at half-past eleven last night in the summerhouse," James reminded her (at the same time setting up a useful point of reference for the untangling of alibis which lay ahead in Act Three).

"That's as may be," Wilhelmina reprimanded him primly. "What a girl does when she's got her uniform on is very different from what she does when she's got it off."

There had been considerable discussion during rehearsal as to whether this was a deliberately funny line and as to how it should be played. The final decision to play it straight was vindicated by total lack of reaction from the Rugland Spa audience, except for a dirty guffaw from a fourteen-year-old boy who hadn't wanted to come but been dragged along to the theatre by his parents.

"Oh, come on," James pleaded.

"No, really, Mr. James. There's you engaged to Miss Kershaw and—"

"She won't mind."

"She'll be a pretty strange fiancée if she doesn't."

"She won't mind, because she won't know. Look, Willy, you know the situation . . ."

In spite of Wilhelmina's rueful nod, James still proceeded with his explanation, because, although she might know the situation, the audience did not. "The old man's money only comes to me if I'm married when he pops off. Now, I know there's no chance of him dying in the near future . . ." (Tragic irony, this, if the audience did but realize it.) "On the other hand, I don't want to get caught on the hop, so it'll be safer if I marry Felicity now just to be sure."

"Huh. I thought you really loved me—but all you want is a bit of skirt."

"I do really love you. But even if I did just want a bit of skirt, my father wouldn't wear it."

This line, which no one had thought of as suspect during rehearsal, was greeted by huge laughter. Anxiety glinted in the eyes of James and Wilhelmina. It intensified as they heard an echoing giggle from behind the door of the tall cupboard by the fireplace.

"He's got this social thing about dangling with tomest—er, tangling with domestics," James fluffed on desperately.

"But surely."

Wilhelmina put a full stop after these two words (which were all that the author had supplied in the script), and the pair of them waited ten seconds until the door opened.

It admitted Lady Hilda De Meaux, who informed them that she had something of enormous importance to impart to her son. On his own.

Wilhelmina made for the door. But before she could reach it (and before Lady Hilda could reveal her secret), Felicity Kershaw appeared through the French windows in tennis whites, complaining that James was jolly lazy and that she was fed up with always looking for his balls in the long grass (another moment which made the recalcitrant fourteen-year-old think that he had perhaps hitherto underestimated the theatre as a medium of entertainment).

The cast all looked nervously at the cupboard door, from behind which another snort of laughter had been heard.

A little idle banter ensued between Lady Hilda and Felicity about how much they could do with a cup of tea, and Wilhelmina was dispatched to make the necessary arrangements. She made for the door.

But her exit was again delayed, this time by the return from their walk of Professor Weintraub, Miss Laycock-Manderley and Colonel Fripp. The Professor, fuzzy in tweed and garlanded with binoculars, cameras and tape-recorder, expressed his hopes for good bird-watching during his stay in the area, stating the intention to try his luck the following day over beyond the pine forest.

Colonel Fripp, moustache and hackles bristling, advised caution. Surely the Professor knew that in the pine forest was a top-secret army research establishment?

No? Really? The Professor feigned surprise. How interesting.

In the ensuing pause Miss Laycock-Manderley suddenly announced that she had returned from their walk early because of a premonition. She was, she explained, psychic, and she was experiencing a strong sense of evil. Something awful was going to happen at Wrothley Grange. The feeling was very powerful. "It's happened to me before," she confided, "in many different ways. But I've never had it like this."

Here was another line to tickle the fourteen-year-old's

sense of humor, and again the cast had cause to look with irritation at the cupboard door. Beneath its make-up, Lady Hilda's face set in an expression of annoyance as she laughed off her guests' fears and once again suggested the cure-all of tea.

James thought this was a jolly good idea, Felicity confessed to being parched, and Professor Weintraub joked heavily about the way everything in England stopped for tea.

Wilhelmina (for whom the Act had now degenerated into a series of frustrated attempts to exit) was once again sent off to fetch tea. She made for the door. But before she reached it, Lady Hilda remembered that they would not have enough tables for so large a party. Would Wilhelmina mind getting one of the folding card-tables out of the cupboard by the fireplace?

"No, of course not, milady," enthused Wilhelmina, glad perhaps of another door to make for.

In the front row of the Circle, the time-freckled hand of Leslie Blatt, the play's author, squeezed the knee of his eighteen-year-old companion. "This bit's good," he wheezed. "Never fails."

Wilhelmina turned the handle of the cupboard and the door swung outwards.

The body of an elderly man in tweeds fell out. It landed neatly on its back in the space between a sofa and an armchair.

Stuck in its chest was a dueling sword. The red light from the window intensified the glistening wet redness on his shirtfront.

The cast, disposed in a neat semicircle around the body, gasped as one.

"Oh no!" screamed Lady Hilda. And then, for purposes of identification, "It's Reginald!" Finally, for those in the audience of particularly slow perception, she added, "Killed by one of his own dueling swords!"

The dueling sword trembled and swayed as the body shook with suppressed giggles.

The curtain fell to a clacking of geriatric applause.

As soon as it was down, Lady Hilda's face lost its last vestige of benevolence. "Bloody unprofessional!" she stormed. "I will not work with people who behave like that. Either he goes or I go!"

And she made for her dressing-room.

In the stalls an old lady fumbled with the cellophane on her box of After-Dinner Mints. "Not much of a part for that actor, the one who dies, is it?" she observed to her companion.

"No," her companion agreed.

"I wonder if it's someone we know from the television."

Her companion turned the pages of her program with arthritic hands. "No, the name doesn't mean anything to me."

"What is it?"

"Charles Paris. You heard of him?"

"No, dear."

CHAPTER
TWO

AFTER THE CURTAIN-CALL Charles Paris tried again to ring his estranged wife, Frances, but again there was no reply.

There were no spirits at the brief first night party, so Charles had to make do with a glass of bitter Spanish red. It was not what he needed, but it was better than nothing. It might dissipate the headache left from the day's earlier excesses. He knew he was weak-willed to react to stress by drinking, but stress had a very debilitating effect on his will. His resolutions to drink less always occurred when he was feeling strong-willed, and at such times he didn't need the support of excessive drinking anyway.

He didn't want to talk to anyone at the party, just to pickle his distress in private, but the theatre's General Manager, Donald Mason, dragged him across to a middle-aged couple who were introduced as Herbie and Velma Inchbald. Donald, who had the incisive manner and affected the pin-striped suits of corporate middle management, was difficult to refuse.

The Inchbalds were well-dressed—possibly over-dressed for the first night of a play at a provincial rep theatre. Herbie, who compensated for his stocky shortness with an

Einstein mane of gray hair and a large cigar, wore a dark velvet suit and a velvet bow-tie, which at first sight gave the impression of evening dress. His wife's pudgy, powdered face was squarely framed by black hair which looked like (and quite possibly was) a wig. The precise definition of her curves was expensively obscured by a blue full-length dress in some ruched semi-transparent material, but the space it took up suggested they were ample. The fat of her neck and fingers was constricted by jewelry.

"Herbie is Chairman of the Theatre Board." Donald Mason supplied this information and bustled off efficiently.

"Ah," said Charles Paris.

"First time you've worked at the Regent, Mr. Paris?"

Yes. If working is the word for what I'm doing, he thought savagely. Does being a dead body count as working? Though of course someone has to play it—can't have non-Equity stiffs crashing the union closed shop.

He contented himself with saying, "Yes."

"Grand little theatre," Herbie Inchbald affirmed complacently. He pronounced the word "thee-ettah," which made Charles' hackles rise. He knew it was mere snobbery, but he could never believe that people who said "thee-ettah" were true friends of the medium.

"Won't find a better little rep for a few hundred miles, I can tell you," Herbie Inchbald continued. "No, people come a long way to see our little shows."

"From as far away as Leominster," Velma Inchbald agreed. "Even some from Worcester."

"Ah."

"Do you know Herefordshire well, Mr. Paris?"

"Not very, no."

"You'll find it's a lovely county."

"Oh, good."

The conversation seemed about to go under for the third time. Charles handed it a straw to clutch at. "Did you enjoy the show tonight?"

Under normal circumstances modesty would have stopped him from asking the question, but he felt that the size of his contribution to this particular production absolved him from any charges of fishing for compliments.

"Oh, yes, grand show."

"Grand," Velma agreed.

Charles wondered whether his hearing was going, along with other waning faculties like hoping, coping and bladder control. Could it really be that they had enjoyed *The Message Is Murder*? He hadn't spent very long rehearsing the piece, because of the nature of his part, but it had been long enough to form the opinion that the play was the direst piece of codswallop ever to be exhumed from the mortuary of dead plays.

"You mean you thought it was well done?" This seemed marginally more likely than that they had actually enjoyed the writing.

"Well done, and a damned good little play."

"Yes, a good little play," echoed Velma.

Charles must have failed to disguise his disbelief, because he found himself being asked if he didn't like the piece.

"Well, erm, it's probably not my favorite sort of play. I mean, I often wonder how plays like that do get chosen. I mean, there are thousands of really good plays around and . . ."

"Herbie helped choose the play."

"Oh. Did he?"

"Yes, I did. Well, credit where it's due. Donald first suggested it. But soon as I read it, I thought it was a grand little play."

"And then you read it again when we were in Corsica in the summer."

"That's right, I did. Still thought it was grand."

"Ah."

"You see, Mr. Paris, in a local rep you have to give the public what they want. All right, maybe *The Message is Murder* isn't experimental, hasn't got any arty-farty pretensions, but it's damned good entertainment. Nothing like a thriller to bring the crowds in—especially if it's got "murder" in the title. And you know, Leslie Blatt's a local author too—retired to Bromyard—so that's another attraction. Oh yes, a good thriller, a Shakespeare, the pantomime, of course—

those are your bankers at a local rep. Those are the sort of things people in Rugland Spa want to see. Get those under your belt and then you can afford to be a bit experimental. I mean, do you know what our next production is . . . ?''

"Yes, I heard."

"*Shove It*, that's what it is. *Shove It*. Now there's a modern play, if you like. Going to raise a few eyebrows in Rugland Spa, isn't it, Velma?''

"I should say so."

"But it's the sort of show we ought to do . . . every now and then. And with Kathy Kitson in it, the people'll come along.''

"Yes . . .''

"We're very proud of the Regent here in Rugland Spa, Mr. Paris.''

"Yes, well, it's a lovely old theatre," said Charles, trying to soften the accusation in Herbie Inchbald's tone.

"Certainly is. Built in 1894, you know. Checkered career, like most theatres. Kept opening and closing under different managements. Closed completely after the last war—sold and used as a repository for corn . . .''

"A tradition that is still maintained," Charles joked ill-advisedly.

"What?"

"Nothing."

"Anyway, virtually derelict in the early sixties, then some farsighted lads on the council took it in hand—all refurbished—reopened in '62."

"And has been going ever since?"

"More or less, yes. Nasty scare, what, three years back? Big offer for the whole Maugham Cross site—that's what this part of the town's called—from a property company. Don't know if you know them—Schlenter Estates?"

"No."

"Oh, well, they're big. Anyway, lot of the council wanted to sell, but we organized local opinion and held on. Close call, though. After that we reconstituted the Board, and I got in Lord Kitestone to be our Patron."

"Oh," said Charles in a way that he hoped sounded

interested. The name had been delivered in a way that required reaction.

"Willie Kitestone owns Onscombe House, stately home out on the Ludlow road," Velma added helpfully. "Very large place."

"Ah . . ."

Once again the conversation lay inert, and Charles tried a tentative kiss of life. "So many provincial theatres these days seem to depend for their survival on the local council."

"Oh yes."

"And the Arts Council, of course."

"Oh yes."

"Still, we're all right here." Velma Inchbald smiled sweetly. "So long as Herbie's on the council. He's a real thee-ettah-lover."

Charles couldn't think of anything to say. He didn't like the Inchbalds and that made him feel guilty. He should have liked them, he should have approved of their support for the theatre, his profession needed more people with their attitude . . . And yet . . . And yet they seemed to him just boring and slightly pompous.

No doubt a reflection of his own mood. But he felt cussedly disinclined to resuscitate the conversation yet again.

Herbie did it for him. "Of course, it's not just me," he said magnanimously, in a voice that seemed to invite contradiction. "A lot of other people help make the Regent a going concern. I mean, you know Donald—he's a real firecracker. Full of ideas. Only been here a year, but he's really made some changes. Bright young man is Donald. I'm always ready to listen to his advice."

"And of course Tony works so hard." Charles felt he should mention the Artistic Director. Though Antony Wensleigh was somewhat vague and a bit of an old woman, there was no questioning his commitment to the Regent Theatre.

"Yes." The word contained less than whole-hearted endorsement from Herbie Inchbald. "Mind you, he'd be lost without Donald. And we have to be careful. This theatre's under constant threat, you know. Prime position in the town. Good few developers like to snap it up. Only take a little bit of

mismanagement for the place to cease to be economically
viable. Then it closes, I get outvoted on the council—there's
plenty of Philistines on that council, you know—and before
you can say knife, the Regent's gone to make way for another
supermarket, or hotel, or what-have-you. And that'd be terrible.''

''Terrible,'' Velma concurred.

After *The Message Is Murder* Charles didn't feel so sure.
And despised himself for the meanness of the thought.

He managed to escape the Inchbalds and get another glass
of the Spanish red, which was tasting increasingly as if the
bottle had been left open for a week. It matched the
sourness of Charles' mood.

He knew its basic cause, but he also knew that it had
been aggravated by the events of the evening. It really hurt
him to have been described as unprofessional by Kathy
Kitson at the end of the first act. And it hurt the more
because he knew the charge was justified. No excuses about
the state of emotional tension he was in could excuse his
childish giggling at the idiocies of Leslie Blatt's dialogue.

As he thought of the playwright, he looked across to the
old man, whose claw-like hands were pawing his eighteen-
year-old companion, trying to dissuade her from her assertion that she really ought to be going home. Charles shuddered.
For a man in his fifties with a taste for young actresses, the
sight of Leslie Blatt prompted unwelcome comparisons.

Still, one thing he could do—indeed, should do—to
regain some of the day's lost ground, was to make his peace
with Kathy Kitson.

He looked across at her. She had changed out of her Lady
Hilda De Meaux costume, but didn't look any different.
Kathy Kitson never looked any different. She was an actress
who lacked the humility Mahomet had shown to the moun-
tain. She didn't go to her parts; they came to her. And if a
few of the lines—or even the whole emphasis—of the play
had to change to accommodate her performance, then that's
the way it had to be.

Kathy Kitson's only performance consisted of Kathy Kitson,
her hair set that afternoon, walking elegantly round stages in

waisted silk dresses, and speaking with brittle elocution
whatever lines she thought appropriate to Kathy Kitson.
This she had done endearingly in West End comedies,
during the fifties, popularly in the television sit com *Really,
Darling?* during the late sixties, and with decreasing *éclat* in
decreasingly prestigious provincial theatres during the seventies and into the eighties. This performance she had
finally brought, with the desperation of the last dodo, to *The
Message Is Murder* at the Regent Theatre, Rugland Spa.

And this performance, to judge from what she was saying to
a young man in a leather jacket as Charles approached, was
the one she intended to give in the forthcoming production of
that searing indictment of contemporary society by one of
Britain's most controversial young playwrights, *Shove It*.

"You see, darling," she murmured huskily. "I don't
think all that . . . language is necessary."

"But," protested the young man in the leather jacket,
"Royston Everett's language is an authentic reflection of life
on the streets of Liverpool."

"I'm sure it is, darling, but one can't just present plays
for the people of Liverpool."

"It's not *for* the people of Liverpool, it's *about* the
people of Liverpool. Everett was brought up in Toxteth. He
knows what he's talking about."

"I'm sure he does, but that is not really the point. You
see, my feeling is that playwrights tend to fall back on bad
language when their confidence is threatened."

"Oh."

"When they're afraid their points won't get across, they
reinforce them with bad language."

"Well—"

"In my young day that wasn't necessary. We used something else to reinforce the playwright's points—an old-
fashioned little thing called *acting*."

This left the young man in the leather jacket without
speech, and gave Charles the opportunity to intervene.
"Kathy, I just wanted to apologize—"

"And another thing I think is unnecessary," she went on,

turning a deep-frozen, silk-clad shoulder to Charles, "is all this nudity."

"Oh, but sometimes," the young man in the leather jacket protested, "it's absolutely essential."

"No, darling." Kathy Kitson's put-down was gentle, but firm. "Again, a good actress can give the impression of nudity while remaining dressed."

In a waisted silk dress, no doubt, Charles thought vindictively. He couldn't really blame her for cutting him, but it didn't improve his mood. He drained his Spanish vinegar and went to replenish it. Ahead of him at the bar were two men, one crumpled, fat and unfamiliar, the other Gordon Tremlett, the actor who had played Colonel Fripp.

The crumpled fat man was persuading the girl behind the bar that it'd save time if she filled him a pint glass of wine rather than "one of these piddling little things." He succeeded, and moved away with the brim of the tankard already to his lips.

Charles could always recognize a professional drinker. "Who is he?" he asked Gordon Tremlett.

"Frank Walby, love. Theatre Critic on the *Gazette*."

"Ah. And what's he going to think of the show?"

"Oh, he'll adore it. Never given a bad notice in his life. Bit like a review in *Stage*—so nice it doesn't mean anything. Praise for all, my dear, including the lady who tore the tickets. No, I've lived in Rugland Spa fifteen years and never seen a harsh word from Frank."

Gordon Tremlett had an unusual history for an actor. He had come into the business after taking an early retirement as, of all things, a bank manager. Always a keen (and talented) amateur actor, he had managed to get his Equity ticket, and worked at the Regent whenever there was a suitable small part for him. He had hardly ever worked anywhere else, but demonstrated the fanaticism of all converts and was far more theatrical than most lifetime actors.

His colleagues regarded him with amused tolerance and occasional resentment. The latter arose whenever he tried to identify too closely with the rest of the company. They could not treat as an equal in their own hazardous profession someone cushioned by a large pension from Barclays Bank.

Gordon Tremlett's talent was serviceable, but he was an example of Antony Wensleigh's tendency to surround himself with casts of friends rather than searching out excellence.

"Sorry, love," Gordon apologized, picking up a tray of drinks and moving off. "Got some people in."

Gordon always had people in. His own little claque, all members of the amateur dramatic society he had formerly supported and now patronized, all still slightly breathless at the fact that one of their number was working in the "real" theatre.

Charles was walking away from the bar with another glass of gall, when Donald Mason again busied up to him.

"Charles," the General Manager whispered. "Just a warning."

"What?"

"Lad in the leather jacket— he's one of the Arts Council assessment team."

"Really?"

"Yes. And our prospects of getting a grant for next season are dicey enough, so just be careful."

"Sure. But you'd better detach him from Kathy. He seems to be a big fan of Royston Everett's work, and she's calmly telling him how she plans to expurgate all her lines in *Shove It*."

"Oh, that's not the sort of thing that's going to worry him. No. I'm more concerned that he doesn't hear about Tony's mismanagement."

"What mismanagement?" It was news to Charles that the Artistic Director had been guilty of any.

"Oh, you know, cock-ups over the budget and all the other things. For God's sake don't let the Arts Council bloke hear about those."

Charles raised his head and, over Kathy Kitson's shoulder, met the eyes of the young man in the leather jacket. There was no doubt that the Arts Council bloke had heard Donald Mason's words.

Mr. Pang, owner of The Happy Friend Chinese Restaurant and Takeaway, watched impassively as Cherry Robson rose from the table, slapped Leslie Blatt round the head and swept out. Cherry, a former dancer now toying with the idea of becoming a straight actress (she was playing Wilhelmina in *The Message Is Murder*), was a tough girl who knew with great accuracy what she wanted from life. It didn't include being touched up by septuagenarian playwrights.

Leslie Blatt, totally unsquashed, leered at Charles. "I'll get her, you know. Women are like that, always say no when they mean yes."

Charles shuddered and returned to his congealing Number Forty-Three. He shouldn't have come to the restaurant. He wasn't hungry. He knew he was only there because he didn't want to be alone yet, and also so that he'd get back too late to catch the appalling tea and curiosity of his landlady, Mimi.

He felt alienated and alone as he looked along the table. Rick Harmer, the young Assistant Stage Manager, appeared to be baiting Leslie Blatt. Rick was a bright boy, who had got the Rugland Spa job straight out of R.A.D.A. When he'd served his forty weeks and got his full Equity ticket, there was no doubt that he would go far. His readings-in for other members of the cast at rehearsal had revealed considerable talent, and he was already signed up with one of the biggest London agencies, Creative Artists Ltd. He treated the Regent Theatre with a slight air of patronage, but, since he did all the many duties required of him with more than the usual efficiency, it was difficult to find fault with him. But his certainty (probably quite justified) that he was going to be a lot more successful than the rest of the company had ever been didn't endear him to his colleagues.

He had also had some success as a writer of comedy sketches for radio and television, and it was with this that he was baiting Leslie Blatt.

"Yes, they're making a radio pilot of one of my scripts in a couple of weeks. Up at the Beeb."

"Beeb?" asked Leslie Blatt, out of touch with such colloquialisms.

"BBC. No, I'll be going up to the recording—ooh, that reminds me, must tell Tony I'll need time off. Only radio, of course, but that'll lead to telly. LWT have got one of my other scripts at the moment. My literary agent . . ." He left a little pause to ensure that the distinction between this figure and his performing agent was not missed. ". . . says they're very keen. Think it might be a good vehicle for Christopher Milton."

"Who?" asked Leslie Blatt, rather testily.

"Haven't you heard of him?" Rick Harmer did not comment further on this ignorance of the entertainment scene. "Has all your work been tatty old thrillers, Leslie?"

The playwright bridled. "What do you mean?"

"I mean, have you done much telly?"

"Not a lot, no," the playwright replied, cautiously dressing up failure to its best advantage. "I'm really a man of the theatre, you know. The theatre and the boudoir . . ."

Further down the table, Laurie Tichbourne, seen earlier in the evening in the tennis kit of James De Meaux, preened himself in the beams of adoration that emanated from the girl beside him. He was one of those people, many—though not all—of whom are actors, who reckon that being born with exceptional good looks excuses them from all further effort in life. Laurie Tichbourne, now in his mid-thirties, had had a perfectly satisfactory career exposing his looks and moderate talent as juve leads in most of the reps in the country. He was well-liked (indeed, there was nothing about him to dislike, unless one wanted something positive, like a decision, out of him) and it was quite possible that one day a casting director would swoop down and carry him off to star in a television series, or even a feature film. It was quite possible. So long as getting the job didn't involve any effort on his part, quite possible.

His current source of adoration was the Regent Theatre's other A.S.M., a girl of quite astonishing prettiness called Nella Lewis. In looks she was the perfect complement to Laurie Tichbourne, though Charles suspected she rather outmatched her escort in seriousness of emotional intent (and intelligence).

"Thing was," Laurie drawled, "they wanted me to dye my hair blond for the part. Can you imagine that, Nella— me with blond hair?"

"No, I can't, Laurie."

"Well, I'd had it done once before, for a day I did on a film, and I knew it made me look an absolute fright. Absolute fright. So I said, come on, I know I'm meant to be a German, but all Germans aren't blond. And if this girl's meant to fall for me, she's not going to fall for me with blond hair."

"So what happened?"

"Oh, the director took my point."

"Oh, good."

Charles wondered how long Nella's intelligence could be curbed by infatuation. Then he became aware of a voice on his left.

"You see, every performance is a political statement. Don't you agree, Charles?"

The voice belonged to Gay Milner, the actress who had played Felicity Kershaw.

Charles gave his usual response to questions about politics in the theatre. "Um . . ."

"No, I mean every part reflects some facet of society, and if you feel that society's got to change, then you can express that in the way you play the part."

Unwisely, Charles decided to pursue this line of thought with her. "But you can't apply that to every play. I mean, take tonight's little epic. *The Message Is Murder* has nothing to do with any society that's ever existed. It's set in its own little cloud-cuckoo-land of country houses and butlers and bodies in the library. You can't make political points when you're acting in something like that."

"Oh, but you can, Charles. If you're committed, you must. I mean, it's more difficult. You know, I was in *Scrag End of Neck* at the Bus Depot."

"Ah." Charles nodded appreciatively, as if he'd heard of the play and the theatre. "Really?"

"Yes. And there of course the political message is overt, so it's that much easier to play. *The Message Is Murder* is more of a challenge."

"Hmm. So what is there in your playing of Felicity Kershaw that makes a political statement?"

"Ah well, you see, she is obviously a representative of the propertied classes."

"Yes, I accept that."

"The small percentage of the population who own a disproportionate amount of the country's wealth."

"Okay."

"So, by making her repellent and untrustworthy, I am sounding a warning to the audience to distrust people of that class."

"Oh." That was why she was doing it. And Charles had thought she was playing it repellent because that was the way Leslie Blatt had written the part, and untrustworthy because of her devious involvement in the murder that had to be revealed in Act Three.

"You see, Charles, the theatre has a vital educational function. It's one of the most persuasive forms of grass-roots agit prop that . . ."

Gay Milner droned on. She was not unattractive. Not sensational like Nella, but she had a certain sexy angularity. And seemed to be unattached. There was a time when Charles would have put up with the political claptrap in the hope of getting somewhere with her, when he'd have talked along, maybe gone back to her digs to pursue some complex crux of socialism, maybe moved aside the coffee cups and tested the reaction to a tentative hand laid on . . . But that time seemed long ago.

He felt desolately miserable.

"Charles, old man."

Antony Wensleigh had come down the table to him and squatted on the floor beside him.

"Yes, Tony?" Charles looked at the Artistic Director. The most noticeable feature of Antony Wensleigh's face was his huge, liquid brown eyes, infinitely mournful, infinitely sensitive. They showed enduring sympathy to his casts through all the squabbles and hiccups of rehearsal. They were the reason that people liked working with him as a director.

And yet, it had to be faced, he wasn't in the front rank of his profession. Though passionately devoted to the theatre, there was about him a certain vagueness, a certain lack of push that deprived his productions of a West End finish. He lived to some extent in a world of his own, happiest in the rehearsal room, surrounded by casts he knew well, uneasy and occasionally by default inefficient in boardroom and administrative office. Herbie Inchbald had been right; someone as frequently abstracted as Antony Wensleigh needed the incisive support of a Donald Mason.

Perhaps part of Tony's trouble was that he had been at the Regent too long. Twelve years in the same job had set him apart from the square dance of movement from rep to rep, which is the only way by which theatrical directors rise in their profession. He was now in his early fifties, an age which made dramatic changes for the better unlikely. And he was cozily settled in Rugland Spa. He had come to regard the job as his for as long as he wanted it, the renewal of his annual contract a mere formality, almost as if he were in a normal job like the rest of humanity. And that attitude, in the world of the theatre, was a potentially dangerous one.

"Thing is, Charles..." The huge eyes looked more mournful than ever, as they did when they had something unpleasant to impart. "Thing is, Kathy was a bit upset..."

"I know, Tony, it was unforgivable of me." No point in making excuses. "One of those ridiculous corpses, where something stupid just suddenly seems funny. And I'm afraid, stuck in that little cupboard, things seem disproportionately funny..."

"Yes, well, it's..."

"Won't happen again, Tony. Promise. Better tomorrow."

"Good. Thanks." Antony Wensleigh stood up with relief, and then articulated the prime motivation of his life. "It's just, you know, I like everyone to be happy."

"Yes. Sure."

Mr. Pang was not so indiscreet as to look pointedly at his watch, but he did come over and ask if anyone would like a sweet. Laurie Tichbourne asked what flavors the "Ice Creams (Various)" on the menu were. Mr. Pang said "Vanilla," so they all agreed they'd just have the bill. Its arrival prompted the customary discussion as to how it should be

divided. Gay Milner produced a calculator and worked it
out. Charles reached into his pocket for his share.

He had just enough. He'd been to the bank that day. Where
had it all gone? In the day's depressed drinking, he realized.

Up to his overdraft limit. Only Wednesday and not paid
again until Friday. Then his agent, bloody Maurice Skellern,
would get his customary ten per cent for doing his customary nothing—shit, no. Maurice had recently, after much
argument, raised his commission to fifteen per cent.

Then he owed Mimi for the digs . . . Oh God, money, too.
To add to his other problems.

He didn't want to, but back at Mimi's, in the brushed nylon
sheets of his single bed, he reread the letter.

Dear Charles,

I don't know how I'm going to say this, but presumably by the end of the letter, I will have managed somehow, so here goes.

I have met someone else.

It sounds corny, but I can't think of any other way of
putting it. His name is David. He is, of all things, a
schools inspector. There are complications.

I am not in a state of bliss, I am in emotional turmoil. I
know that feelings don't cut, they fray, and I am a tangle
of fraying feelings.

I don't know what's going to happen. It's the first time
since you left me that I've had this sort of problem (if
problem's the right word).

I want to see you and talk, though I know that would
only mix me up even more.

I'm sorry, Charles. I am very confused. But I wanted
you to know.

Love,
Frances

CHAPTER
<u>THREE</u>

IN SPITE OF his promise to Antony Wensleigh, Charles Paris was not better the next day. He was worse.

Self-hatred takes many forms. One of the commonest involves publicly bad behavior, as if the sufferer is willing the world's opinion of him to descend to the level of his own.

And that was the form it took that day with Charles. Not only did he again drink too much, he also drank too long, and was not in the theatre when the "half" was called.

This was a serious professional crime. The "half" is a magic moment, half an hour (plus five minutes for safety) before the curtain rises. All members of the company, except for those who have arranged special dispensations because of late entrances, must have checked in by then. If any haven't, then the Stage Management starts to panic and frantic reorganization of understudies begins.

But in a profession which has encompassed drunkards of the stature of George Frederick Cooke (whose life Lord Byron describes as "all green-room and tap-room, drams and the drama—brandy, whiskey-punch, and *latterly*, toddy") and Edmund Kean allowances have frequently been

made. Young A.S.M.s quickly learn which pubs to check
out for actors who have "not noticed the time."

But allowances that might be made for stars are less likely
to be made for actors playing dead bodies in tatty thrillers.
And Charles had compounded his felony by deliberately not
drinking in the pub round the back of the Regent (so much
an annex that bells sounded there at the end of the inter-
vals). Instead, he had sought to match his mood by searching out a hotel by the station, which was as seedy as
anything could be in as genteel a place as Rugland Spa.

He knew what he was doing. It was part of a course in
self-abasement, a need for some violent purgation, a flushing-
out of all the pained confusion in his mind. There was no
conviviality, just pointless, solitary drinking—a gesture which,
even as he made it, he knew to be ineffective. Those for
whom it was intended would not see it; and those who did
see would misinterpret it.

And he hadn't even the courage to make the gesture total.
Having guiltily braved out the half, he found his resolve
weakening. The show went up at seven forty-five. His
hopes of being dramatically oblivious of time were not
realized. At twenty past seven he decided not to have
another drink. And twenty-five past found him lumbering
uncomfortably through the quiet terraces of Rugland Spa
towards the Regent Theatre.

He was lucky in that there was no one by the Stage Door
when he lurched in. It was after twenty to eight, Act One
Beginners would have been called and be waiting in the
wings for the curtain to rise. The Stage Manager would be
on the desk, ready to cue lights, and the A.S.M.s would
also be busy. A furtive hope, worthy of a truant schoolboy,
crept into Charles' mind, that he might yet get away with it.
If he went up to his dressing room quickly, got into his
costume and slipped into his cupboard, nobody might notice. After all, he was only the body; probably no one had
bothered to check whether he was there or not.

He grasped the banister of the stairs to the dressing rooms
and pulled himself upwards. The movement seemed bigger

than he had expected; he swung round against the wall, which made him realize just how drunk he was.

As he swayed there, he heard the panicky clatter of shoes coming down the stairs. Round the corner of the flight Nella Lewis appeared at full speed. Her face was flushed and frightened. In her hand she clutched a dueling sword. It was the one produced as Sir Reginald De Meaux's murder weapon in Act Two.

"Oh!" she panted, screeching to an ungainly halt. "Charles!"

"Yes," Charles confirmed, though his tongue, suddenly too big for his mouth, seemed to distort the word.

"You're terribly late."

A nod of the head to confirm this was easier than words.

"We've been in a terrible panic. All kinds of people were going to replace you."

"Sall righ', though. I can do it now."

"Are you sure?" Nella didn't sound convinced.

"Of course. I'm absolutely in control." To emphasize this point. Charles—unwisely, as it turned out—let go of the banister and made an expansive gesture of insouciance. At the same moment the concrete steps seemed to be filched from under him, and he crumpled to an ungainly heap at the foot of the stairs.

"No," said Nella decisively, skipping over him. "You can't go on in that state."

'I've only got to be a dead body, for God's sake," the heap on the floor complained.

But the young A.S.M. was adamant. "No. We'd better stick to the plan we've made. He . . . he . . ." Her voice was strained with emotion. "That bastard had better go on for you."

"But I—"

"I've got to go. Curtain up in a second, and I'm on the book tonight." Then, with surprising gentleness, she said, "You need to get back to your digs. I'll organize a cab for you when I've got a moment."

She scuttered off.

Charles lay there. Everything around him seemed to be

moving; only the contempt he felt for himself remained immovable in his mind.

Had it really come to this? Fifty-five years of development reduced to an alcoholic mess on the stone floor. A career washed away by booze, a marriage—

The thought of Frances stopped him short like a blow in the face. Whatever their relationship, what he was doing now wasn't helping it. No, he must pick himself up, not succumb to self-pity and its attendant alcohol. He had a job to do and he would do it.

With great concentration he pulled himself to his feet and walked very carefully up to the first landing, where there was a men's lavatory. He filled the sink with cold water and splashed it copiously over his face.

It made him feel a very little better. He walked cautiously along to the next flight of stairs, and found himself confronted by Leslie Blatt.

The elderly playwright looked extremely guilty. Charles wondered what he had been doing. Most of the actresses had their dressing rooms on the floor above. Charles wouldn't put it past the old goat to have been doing a bit of keyhole-peeping.

But he was in no position to be censorious. As Leslie Blatt wasted no time in telling him.

"Oh, Charles, everyone's been looking for you."

"I know," Charles said wearily.

"I was going to go on for you."

"You?"

"Yes. I used to be an actor and director, you know, before I started writing. Kept my card up. Always ready to do the odd little bit." He sniggered, somehow infecting this remark with unwholesome innuendo.

"Yes. Well, as you see, I'm here now. So it won't be necessary for you to—"

"Oh, I'm not going to now," said Leslie Blatt petulantly. "No, I've just been told I mustn't, by young Mr. Smartypants. Says it's his job. Huh." The old man tossed his wrinkled head.

"Oh, well, I—"

"No, he's going to do it. He's arranged it all. So you'd just better go home and sober up."

"And what are you going to do?"

"I'm going to watch my play from backstage. Always enjoy that. Get a completely different set of thrills backstage." The playwright stalked off, once again giving an unpleasantly sexual overtone to his final remark.

Inside his dressing room Charles discovered who Leslie Blatt had meant by "young Mr. Smartypants." Rick Harmer, dressed in the late Sir Reginald De Meaux's tweeds, was sitting in front of the mirror, about to apply make-up.

"Charles!" he said. "You're terribly late."

Charles was getting sick of people stating the obvious. "Yes, I am."

"And you're pissed."

"Again, yes, I am."

"You'd better go home. You can't act in that state."

"Dead bodies don't have to act," Charles argued belligerently.

"No, but they have to keep still. You can't have a dead body lying there with an attack of D.T.s."

"I haven't got D.T.s. I'll be fine. Now please could I have my costume."

"As A.S.M., Charles, I'm understudying all the male parts. And if someone isn't in by the half, then—"

"Rick, please."

The appeal contained just enough dignity to prevent it from being abject, and Rick responded to its nakedness.

"Okay," he said, as he started to unbutton the tweeds. "I shouldn't really, but okay."

"Thank you." With great caution, uncertain of his balance, Charles started to take his clothes off.

He tried desperately to think of something to say, something that might make the situation seem normal, something that would remove the expression, half of pity, half contempt, from the young man's face. "How are things going with your radio pilot?" he finally managed.

"Oh, okay. Got a good cast together. Toby Root, Anna Duncan . . . you worked with either of them?"

"Yes. Long time ago." The second name stirred memories that Charles did not wish to exhume further.

"And George Birkitt's very keen. But his agent's shilly-shallying over money."

"Ah."

"Only trouble is, that bastard Wensleigh won't release me for the day to go up to the recording."

"Really? That's most unlike Tony."

"Don't you believe it," said Rick bitterly. "He likes to play the little Hitler. Jealousy, really. Typical of someone who's over the hill and knows it."

The A.S.M. used that as an exit line, and Charles didn't feel he was being unduly sensitive in including himself in its application. Nor could he really feel that the aspersion was without justification.

He turned up the loudspeaker in the dressing room. Onstage James De Meaux was still reminiscing to Wilhelmina about what they had got up to in the summerhouse the previous evening, so he had plenty of time. Laboriously, he got into his costume and did his make-up. The latter took a depressingly short time; to look sixty-five all Charles had to do was gray his temples and stick on a gray moustache; to look dead all he had to do was powder his cheeks down to a horrid pallor (and the way he looked that evening even these minimal changes seemed superfluous).

Then he remembered he was meant to be impaled by a dueling sword. If he had omitted that, he would really have finished the evening. He imagined Kathy Kitson bringing down the curtain on the First Act with the lines, "Oh no! It's Reginald! Killed by some method that is not immediately apparent!"

The thought made him giggle weakly. No, no, mustn't do that. No corpsing tonight. He was already in enough trouble. With uncoordinated fingers, he started to remove his jacket and shirt.

The device for his apparent transfixation had been improvised by Nella Lewis in the props room, and was simple but effective. A broad elastic belt, of the type that used to be called "waspee" (though that description was singularly inappropriate when it was buckled round Charles' chest), had a thin block of wood stapled to the front of it, and through this block a bolt had been fixed to stick out at right angles. The shirt was buttoned around this protuberance, and a foreshortened dueling sword with specially adapted end was screwed on to it. The area of the wound was then sprinkled liberally with stage blood (known in the business as "Kensington Gore"), and the effect, even from close quarters, was surprisingly convincing.

With gloomy intimations of mortality, Charles surveyed his dead body in the mirror. Then he made his way unsteadily down on to the stage.

But before he could reach the sanctuary of his cupboard, he walked into Tony Wensleigh. Rick Harmer's description of a "little Hitler" was most inappropriate; at that moment the anxiety on the Artistic Director's face made him look more like the White Rabbit.

Unfortunately, having bumped, Charles overcompensated to regain his balance, and again found himself on the floor. Tony Wensleigh bent down to pick him up.

"Charles," he whispered sadly, "you can't go on in that state."

"I can, Tony. Be all right. Honestly."

"No. Donald told me what had happened, and I've just seen Rick, who said you're completely pie-eyed."

"I'm not, Tony. Just a bit pie-eyed. And I'm very sorry."

"That's not the point now. Look, Charles, you know I don't like coming the heavy, but I've got to think of the play. You could ruin it."

Charles bit back the retort that Leslie Blatt seemed to have done that already.

"No, I've decided. I've told Rick. I'm going to go on for you."

"You?"

"Yes. Rick's needed backstage. Nella's not experienced enough to cope without him."

"But, Tony..."

"No, Charles. Sorry, it's nothing personal, but I'm responsible for the show and I can't afford to take risks. I have my position as Artistic Director to think of."

The drink was now making Charles belligerent. "Oh, don't be so bloody pompous!"

"I am not being pompous. Listen, the Chairman of the Board's in the theatre tonight. I can't run the risk of you ruining the show."

"But—"

"I'm sorry, Charles, but my mind's made up and nothing's going to shift me."

"For God's sake, Tony..." The drink was also making him unusually pertinacious and eloquent. "Look, what threat am I to you? What harm can one slightly drunken middle-aged actor do to your "position as Artistic Director"? What do you think I'm going to do—expose you, denounce you to the Board, reveal a long history of fraud and peculation?" He paused after this flight of rhetorical hyperbole. "All I'm going to do is go on stage and be a dead body. I haven't even got any lines to cock up. Please, Tony. Please let me do it."

At this point Tony Wensleigh gave a classic demonstration of his qualities as a decision-maker. "Okay, Charles," he said. "You go on. But don't show me up."

What appeared from the auditorium to be the interior of a cupboard was a little niche made of two small flats. The third side, invisible from out front, was not there, allowing easy access for dead bodies. But space backstage was so cramped by the large box-set of Wrothley Grange that Charles had to spend most of the act in position. And once inside the cupboard, its miserly proportions offered him the alternatives of standing bolt upright against the back flat or sitting with his legs twisted through the cleats and stage weights that supported the set. Charles had always found standing preferable.

The flats of the cupboard were old and had been used many times. On the back of one was scribbled "Uncle Vanya—Act Two," on the other "When We Are Married—L.

Fireplace,'' and these scrawls perhaps reflected their original provenance. But the stretched canvas had been repainted many times and many colors since then, and contributed to a wide variety of theatrical experiences.

The feel of the thick paint was comfortingly familiar against Charles' hands, as he stood against the back wall of his cupboard. Must stand, mustn't lean, he kept telling himself. His full weight could easily overtopple a flat and, since most of the others were nailed together with lathes at the top, might easily bring down more. He had already done enough wrong that evening; he didn't want to add the total collapse of Wrothley Grange to his misdemeanors.

But he did want to lean against something. The uncontrollable phase of his drunkenness had passed, to be replaced by a deep, deep tiredness. The heat of the stage lights through the canvas door before him, the familiar backstage smells of sawdust, size and dusty drapes, and the relentless banalities of Leslie Blatt's dialogue, all contributed to his fatigue. He just wanted to go to sleep.

If he just closed his eyes for a little . . . just for a little, he wouldn't miss his cue. He closed them, then opened them again with a start as he lurched against the back of his cupboard.

No, be safer if he sat down. Just for a minute. Professor Weintraub was still going on about bird-watching, so he'd be safe for a little doze. Just a little doze . . .

A noise very close woke him. A strange noise, a sudden ripping, a tearing of cloth. It seemed to come from just above his head.

He looked up, blinking in the darkness. But even as he did so, he heard Lady Hilda De Meaux asking her maid if she'd mind getting one of the folding card-tables out of the cupboard by the fireplace.

"No, of course not, milady," Wilhelmina replied, and the door of Charles' sanctum swung open, flooding him with light.

And in that light he saw something sticking through the flat at the back of the cupboard.

Then he saw Wilhelmina's startled face looking down at

him, and realized that his recumbent position was totally obscured from the audience by a large sofa.

Instinctively trying to save the act, he leapt up with a throttled cry, staggered forward to his correct dying position and fell with what he thought was not a bad death-rattle.

It was only as he lay still and heard the edge in Kathy Kitson's voice pronouncing the curtain-line that he realized he had completely buggered up the play's plot. Professor Weintraub was going to need a great deal of confidence to make his assertion in Act Two that, from his examination of the corpse, it was clear that Sir Reginald had been dead for at least eight hours. Oh dear, more recrimination.

There certainly was, plenty, as soon as the curtain fell. Kathy Kitson was the most vociferous, but none of the cast showed much charity to Charles.

He hardly noticed. He let the abuse wash over him. His mind was fixed elsewhere.

It was fixed on what he had seen at the back of his cupboard when the door opened. Clear in the light, before it was hastily withdrawn, he had seen the sharp blade of the prop dueling sword.

It had been thrust with some force through the canvas of the flat from backstage.

And, but for the drunken lapse which had moved Charles from his usual position, the sword would have gone straight through him.

CHAPTER
<u>FOUR</u>

"COURSE, I'VE HAD drunks before..." Mimi drew her pale green candlewick housecoat round her with the confidence of a woman for whom the world could hold no surprises. "Oh, yes, lot of my gentlemen been drunks."

Charles grunted. At half-past nine in the morning the last thing he wanted to hear about was Mimi's "gentlemen."

"Mind you, real drunks they was, most of them. I mean, drunks on the grand scale."

So even his drunkenness was to be disparaged. Mimi was capable of disparaging anything. Why, not for the first time Charles asked himself, did he never end up with the theatrical landladies one always heard about, the "treasures," the motherly ones, the ones for whom no trouble was too great? They did exist, they must exist—too many actors talked about them for their existence to be complete fiction. There were even, if the stories were to be believed, *sexy* landladies, whose bed and breakfast were really worth having.

But Charles Paris never ended up with them; he always got the Mimis of this world, the censorious, the resentful, the mean, the ... God, Mimi couldn't even cook. He looked down with distaste at waxy eggs which had brought half the frying pan with them, and wooden fried bread which had brought the other half. A pair of tomatoes shriveled like used condoms. And her tea . . . Some vital ingredient seemed to have been omitted from its making. Tea, perhaps.

Granted, he was not in much of a state to appreciate any food. Nausea bobbed like an extra uvula in his throat. But even in that condition he could recognize the true horror of Mimi's culinary efforts.

"One drunk I had—Everard Austick. You met him?"

"Yes."

"Now he was a drunk. Completely lost his senses when he'd had a skinful. Came home one night so drunk he told me I couldn't cook. Imagine that."

"Yes."

"Said I cooked like an Irish laborer mixing cement."

"Ah."

"Didn't mean it, of course. Ate up his scrambled eggs like a lamb the next morning."

That's what made Mimi so difficult to deal with—her unassailable confidence. Whatever was said to her, whatever complaint about her sloppy housekeeping, she seemed impervious. Worse than that, she took everything as a compliment. Her self-image remained perfectly intact. She saw herself as the lovable figure of the theatrical landlady who always eluded Charles.

"Always comes back, Everard Austick, when he's working Rugland Spa. All my gentlemen always come back. It's like home from home with you, Mimi, that's what they all say."

God, thought Charles, a lot of actors are supposed to have depressing home lives, but not many of them could be that bad.

And yet what she said seemed to be true. She kept a visitors' book, and Charles had not escaped scanning its pages. And there was the evidence—names, dates, comments—"Just like being back with Mum," "Ee, you spoil me, Mimi," "Lovely as always" . . . Did she practice some mass sorcery on her victims? Or had her very first theatrical gentleman lost his nerve and, by putting something nice in the visitors' book, embarrassed all his successors into doing the same?

Charles was determined that, when his stay was up, he

would write exactly what he really thought of Mimi's hospitality. But, even as he had the thought, he felt his conviction drain away and knew that he would succumb like all the others to smirking insincerity.

"Oh yes, I seen drunks," she reiterated. "All the famous ones stay with Mimi. Ask specially to stay with Mimi. Because, you see, they know I'll never pass judgment, never tell them how contemptible they are."

With this, she flashed Charles a look of withering judgment and total contempt.

"Oh yes, they all stay with Mimi. You name them, they've stayed with me."

"George Frederick Cooke?" Charles hazarded maliciously.

"Oh yes, he always comes. Whenever he's in the area he pops in to see Mimi."

Another of Mimi's little charms was name-dropping. Whoever was mentioned, she knew them; and if discussion ensued, she knew them better than the person she was talking to.

"What about Edmund Kean?" Charles continued recklessly. "Has he stayed with you?"

"Just the once," said Mimi tartly. Then she again looked sharply at her guest. "Oh, did I say—there was a telephone message for you?"

"No, you didn't."

"From the General Manager at the theatre."

"Oh."

"I didn't wake you. Told him you was sleeping it off."

"Thank you very much, Mimi."

"Think nothing of it. Anything for my gentlemen." She gave a sickly smile, as usual obscuring whether she was aware or not of her own ironies. "Anyway, he wants you to go and see him."

No surprise, really, thought Charles. Long time since I've been sacked. The prospect gave him a perverse pleasure; it was the logical culmination of the previous day's kamikaze behavior.

"When does he want to see me?"

"Soon as convenient, he said."

"I'd better go straight away." Charles rose.
"Oh no, you've got time to finish your eggs."
Charles sank back into his chair.

The administrative office was at the top of the Regent
Theatre, above the bar. When Charles entered, it was empty.
The room, snatched out of storage space as an afterthought,
was cramped but, compared to most of the theatre administrative offices he had seen, well-organized. Its tidiness, he
thought, probably reflected the mind of the General Manager. Donald Mason, it seemed, had been with the Regent less
than a year, but had made a quick impression on the
efficiency of the theatre. His predecessors, according to
Gordon Tremlett, who knew about such things, had been, to
a man, creatures devoted to the principle of minimum effort.

An in-tray and an out-tray were neatly aligned on the
desk, with a telephone and intercom placed exactly between
them. The in-tray was empty, a commendable sign of
industry at that time in the morning. The out-tray was fairly
full, and on top of it was a handwritten note.

The writing was recognizably tiny. Charles had received a
good-luck note in the same hand on the opening night of
The Message Is Murder.

He couldn't read the note in the in-tray without crossing
the room to peer at it. Which he knew he shouldn't do.

But which, with the recklessness of a man about to lose
his job, he did.

The note read as follows:

> "SORRY ABOUT THE TOTAL COCK-UP
> OF EVERYTHING. NO EXCUSES.
>   YOURS ABJECTLY,
>   TONY"

Oh dear. What was the Artistic Director's latest feat of
mismanagement?

Charles heard a movement outside the door and moved
hastily across to the other side of the room. Donald Mason

entered in another of his executive suits, looking grimly flustered.

"Sorry, Charles, won't keep you a minute. One important call I must make." The General Manager dialed without disturbing the symmetry of the telephone's position on his desk. "Ah, Mr. Hughes. Donald Mason here, Regent Theatre. Just checking the position on the Drill Hall. Yes, yes, that's what I heard. Hmm. No, of course I can see your point of view." The General Manager sighed. "Oh yes, I did mention it to him, but it must have slipped his mind. Yes, well, he's got a lot on his plate, particularly when he's in rehearsal for a show. Yes, I agree, he always *does* seem to be in rehearsal for a show. Well, we must make allowances, mustn't we? The old artistic temperament, eh? What? Oh, yes. Anyway, no hard feelings on my side, Mr. Hughes. You gave us plenty of warning and, if it's booked, it's booked. Okay, sorry again. 'Bye."

He put the phone down and looked at Charles with a grim smile. "Sometimes, you know, I feel like one of those men who follows a big parade with a shovel and cleans up after the horses. Except it's a one-man parade that goes by the name of Antony Wensleigh."

"Ah." Charles didn't feel he could comment on the Artistic Director's behavior.

"Know what he's done now? Only lost us the Drill Hall for rehearsals. Caretaker told us weeks ago the Badminton Club wanted to book it, but he'd hold it for us so long as he got written confirmation. Which he didn't get—and guess who should have done it?" He sighed. "So now we'll have to get somewhere else as of the week after next, and that's going to cost us more, and once again the budgeting all goes up the spout and . . . Still, I shouldn't burden you with my problems."

"No." Then Charles volunteered, "I rather assume that I have problems of my own."

"Yes. So you know why I've asked you to come here."

Oh God. The interview was beginning to sound like something out of a Billy Bunter school story. Charles wondered whether he should have stuffed a newspaper down the back of his trousers.

Donald Mason looked at his out-tray. Seeing Tony Wensleigh's note, he casually picked it up, folded it and put it in his inside pocket. No need to advertise the Artistic Director's lapses. He then picked up the next piece of paper from the tray. "I've had a report from the Stage Manager about your behavior during last night's performance."

"Yes."

"You were late for the 'half,' and then, when it came to the moment—and I use the word advisedly—of your performance, you did not play your part as rehearsed, and the general opinion seems to have been that you were . . ."

Charles finished the sentence for him. "Smashed out of my mind."

"Yes." The General Manager paused. "A lot of people would regard such behavior as grounds for dismissal."

"Yes."

"I've talked to Tony about it, and he says there's no question about it—you should go."

"Yes."

"You're just contracted for the one show?"

"That's right." Oh, for God's sake, get on with it. "And my role is hardly onerous. It won't be difficult to get someone else rehearsed up to take over."

"No."

Oh, get on with it. What else is there to say? But Donald seemed hesitant. It was unlikely that someone with his abrasive manner would have difficulty in sacking an actor, but maybe he was finding it awkward. Charles decided to help him out.

"Obviously I'm sorry for the trouble I caused, but I fully understand that you have no alternative but to show me out and—"

"Oh, I wouldn't say that."

Donald Mason's words were so unexpected that Charles gaped at him.

"No, Charles, there are alternatives." Then, with surprising gentleness, the General Manager continued. "People usually have a reason for getting drunk. What is it—domestic problems?''

''Well . . .''

''Woman?''

For a second Charles felt tempted to spill it all out, to succumb to pathos, to plead for sympathy. But, hell, no. He couldn't define the situation with Frances to himself, let alone spell it out to a stranger. ''No, I just got drunk. I sometimes go on these benders. I know it's unprofessional and stupid, but . . .'' He shrugged.

''Hmm. My inclination, Charles, is always to give people a second chance.'' This again seemed inconsistent with Donald Mason's brusque image. ''If you want to stay, I'm prepared to ignore Tony's opinion and let you. What do you say?''

Charles felt embarrassingly emotional. ''Well, I . . . er . . .''

''I mean I'm sure it's not the sort of thing that's going to happen again.''

This was once more back to the headmaster's study. *I'm going to give you one more chance, Paris, and I'm going to trust you, because in my experience most chaps respond to trust.*

''So tell me, do you want to stay in the show?''

''Well, yes, I would be very grateful if . . .'' Mumble, mumble, grovel, grovel.

''Good, that's settled then.'' The General Manager screwed up the Stage Manager's report and threw it into his waste paper basket. ''You know, I think part of the trouble for you is that you've got so little to do in this show.''

''You mean I get drunk on the idle hands principle?''

''Maybe. I think we should try to get you more involved in the company. Perhaps there'll be a part in another of our forthcoming productions.''

''Well, that'd be very . . .''

''I'll see what I can do.''

At that moment the intercom on Donald's desk buzzed and a female voice crackled, ''Mrs. Feller in the foyer. She wants to come and see you about *Shove It*.''

''Oh God. Okay, send her up.'' Donald Mason rose from

his desk and straightened his tie. "Have you come across the redoubtable Mrs. Feller, Charles?"

"No."

"You will. She's Rugland Spa's answer to Mrs. Whitehouse. A one-woman Puritan Backlash, who only comes to the theatre to count the number of letters in the words."

"So she isn't going to care for *Shove It.*"

"No. There'll be protest meetings, picketings, strong letters to the local paper . . . Honestly, what a bloody stupid choice of play for Rugland Spa. Over half the population's past retirement age—they're hardly going to lap up the Anglo-Saxon diatribes of Royston Everett."

"The theatre's got to do some modern stuff."

"Modern, yes, but it doesn't have to be obscene. I sometimes think Tony's judgment has gone completely. He's just lost touch with reality." He shook his head ruefully. "Still, again not your problem, Charles. Anyway, with regard to you, we'll leave things as they are—Okay?"

"Yes. Thank you very much."

"And if Tony—"

Donald Mason was interrupted by a knock on the door. "That'll be Mrs. Feller. This is obviously the early stage of her campaign—she still bothers to knock. It'll get worse."

He extended his hand to the actor. "Thanks for coming in, Charles. I'm relying on you, so keep it up."

Considering the circumstances, Charles reflected, the General Manager's final cliché was singularly inapposite.

Well-being flooded through Charles. Partly it was the first symptom of recovery from his hangover, that breakthrough moment when continuing existence first seems a possibility. When he had woken, three hours previously, the movement from horizontal to vertical had seemed insuperable, and yet here he was, on two feet, moving around, suffering from nothing worse than a light headache playing around his temples. He was even feeling hunger, a sensation which he thought had abandoned his body forever.

He went into a little cafe near the theatre and tucked into an espresso coffee and two jam doughnuts.

Of course the euphoria wasn't just physical. The interview with Donald Mason had contributed enormously. Though he'd thought he'd wanted the catharsis of dismissal, he was deeply relieved to have been spared it. Basically he had a respect for his profession and was disgusted by his unprofessional behavior.

And the surprise of how he had misjudged the General Manager's character added an extra glow.

All he had to do was to behave impeccably for the remainder of the run of *The Message Is Murder*.

And sort out where he stood with Frances.

There was a pay-phone in the cafe. But there was still no reply from his wife's number at her new flat in Highgate.

Still, she was unlikely to be there at twelve o'clock in the morning. If it was term-time, she'd be hard at work at the school where she was headmistress. And if it was half-term or holiday . . . oh God, he could never remember when they came. Frances' life was always sliced up into neat segments by these academic dividers, while his own remained a shifting morass without any demarcation.

He contemplated trying the school, but rejected the idea. Even if she was there, she was bound to be busy, and the circumstances wouldn't be ideal for the sort of conversation they needed to have.

Instead he rang the Pangbourne number of his daughter, Juliet.

She answered.

"It's me . . . Charles." She never called him by his Christian name, but he couldn't bring himself to say "Daddy."

"Oh, hello. How are you?"

"Fine." The conventional lie. "And you?"

"Yes, fine. Busy, but fine."

"Kids?"

"Twins are at school, thank God, but Sebastian's being a bit of a pain. He's teething."

Charles had forgotten about his third grandson, Sebastian, born some eight months previously, "a brother for Damian and Julian." God, why did they choose those names? Probably because Juliet's husband, rising star of the insurance world, had discovered there were special reduced premiums for people whose names ended in I-A-N.

"How is Miles?"

"Oh, fine. He's just been promoted. He's now an Assistant Branch Manager."

"Oh." Then, because comment seemed appropriate. "Good for him."

"Yes, it is. It means we've been able to get a new dishwasher."

"Oh, good."

"Makes a big difference."

"Yes."

"And Miles has just bought me a food-processor, which is going to be a great help mashing up Sebastian's stuff."

"I'm sure it is." He had to change the subject before he was treated to a complete inventory of the Taylersons' kitchen. "I've been trying to contact your mother."

"Ah." He was sure Juliet's tone changed with this syllable. It became more guarded. What was she hiding? Had she been given specific instructions from Frances as to how to deal with inquiries? Had Frances moved into some love-nest with her schools inspector and was Juliet the guardian of their secret address?

"Can't get any reply from her flat."

"No. Well, it's half-term. She's away."

"I thought you said your boys're at school," said Charles with involuntary suspicion.

"Yes, but they have different half-terms from the State schools."

My, oh my. Miles was doing well. Private education. No doubt paid for by a carefully selected insurance policy.

"Of course. When's Frances back?"

"Sunday afternoon, I think." The "I think" was mere dressing; Juliet obviously knew the exact hour of her mother's return.

"Where is she?"

"Paris."

"Ah."

Silence hung between them, the old silence of poor

communication and ungainly love, but now shadowed by another awkwardness.

Charles couldn't just let the conversation drift to more kitchenalia and then goodbyes. He had to ask the question hovering between them.

"Is she there on her own?"

"No."

He must mention the name as if it were familiar, as if he were a man of the world accepting the *fait accompli*. "Is she there with David?" he asked, begging for a negative reply.

"Yes," said Juliet.

In some ways it made things better. At least it introduced an element of definition. Like a condemned man who has heard his sentence, Charles could begin to plan, devise ways of coping with his situation. He ordered another cup of coffee.

It had been inevitable and he had no right to complain. He had left Frances twenty years before, and had been lucky to retain her as an emotional long-stop for so long. There had been rapprochements and reconciliations, but none had lasted. His character and his life were not compatible with the regularities of marriage. The only surprise was that she, still an attractive woman in her early fifties, had not met anyone else sooner.

So he reasoned it out.

But it still hurt.

It was by forcing his mind off the subject of Frances that he began to think about the events of the previous night. His worries about her, the haze and pains of alcohol, the threat of dismissal, had prevented him from concentrating on the rather significant fact that someone had tried to kill him.

Some of his recollections of the night were blurred, but the sight of the sword-blade stabbing through the flat above him was cinematically clear.

It had happened. There was no doubt about it. When he inspected the flat under the working lights of the stage,

Charles could see the new gash in the canvas. He stood in his normal dead body position and confirmed that gash corresponded with the middle of his back. He shivered.

He went round the back of the flat and found that the tear had been repaired. A rectangular strip of canvas had been glued on to prevent the split from spreading. Someone had made that repair, but had it been just an act of routine maintenance or the cover-up of a failed crime?

The theatre appeared to be empty. It was lunchtime on the Friday of the first week of the run. The *Shove It* cast would be at their outside rehearsal room (the Drill Hall which, he had learned that morning, they were about to lose). Any stage staff who might be in the theatre were likely to be up in the bar. But Charles did a little backstage tour to see if he could find the mysterious flat-repairer.

He heard a voice as he approached the Green Room. It was Rick Harmer's. Charles stopped out of sight of the phone and listened.

"Yes, I know that's the situation at the moment, but don't worry, I'm going to be up for that recording. And the whole day's rehearsal. I'm going to see that the cast says my lines *right*. Look, I know that, and I'm not going to risk losing the job here, but somehow I'm going to make the bastard change his mind and agree to release me. I don't know how, I'll think of something. He is not going to stand in my way. No, okay, leave it with me. yes. Anything else come up? Any inquiries? Availability checks?"

These last questions identified Rick's interlocutor as his agent. And Charles gained unworthy pleasure from the fact that Rick obviously got the same answers as he did when making the same inquiries of Maurice Skellern.

He waited till the phone was down before proceeding casually round the corner.

"Oh, Rick. Hello."

"Hi. Feeling better this morning?" the A.S.M. asked with a hint of malice.

"Yes, thank you."

"Seen Donald?"

No secrets in a provincial theatre company.

"Yes. Yes I have." Charles deliberately delayed gratify-
ing Rick's patent curiosity, before saying, "I'm staying
on."

"Oh." The A.S.M. was so surprised it was a moment
before he managed to say, "Good."

"Yes. Oh, incidentally, Rick, I was just looking onstage . . . at the scene of my disgrace . . ."

"Yes?"

"And I noticed there was a tear in the flat at the back of
my cupboard."

"Oh yes, I noticed that. I just repaired it, so that it
doesn't spread."

The answer came quickly enough, and apparently without
guile.

"Any idea how it happened?"

"What?"

"The tear. What I mean is—did I do it while I was
thrashing around last night?"

"Oh, I don't think so. No, I imagine something fell
against it or someone caught a prop on it in the dark."

Which sounded reasonable enough—to anyone who hadn't
seen the real cause.

Charles justified having a pint at lunchtime on medical
grounds. It wasn't going to be the start of another heavy
day; it was just a necessary compensation for the dehydra-
tion caused by his hangover.

And it did taste good.

As he sat over it, he concentrated his mind on the
stabbing.

Two things seemed clear. First, that it had been a deliberate act. And, second, that he had not been the intended
victim.

The second conclusion came from lack of motivation. He
had hardly been in the company long enough for anyone to
build up murderous resentment against him, and the one
person who might harbor such thoughts, Kathy Kitson, had
been onstage at the moment of the attack.

Leslie Blatt had been pretty furious with him the previous

evening for "making nonsense of my play" (no very difficult task, in Charles' view). But the unwitting sabotage of
the plot of *The Message Is Murder* had come after the
stabbing, so could not be claimed as motivation.

Nor were there any young ladies in the company who
might (as in many other companies in which he had worked)
have been offended by amorous advances from Charles
Paris. His state of confusion over Frances had prevented him
from even being aware of other women.

No, whoever had wielded the dueling sword was under
the impression that someone else was playing the late Sir
Reginald De Meaux. And there was no shortage of candi-
dates for the corpse's job. Practically every male in the
company who wasn't actually onstage at the end of Act One
seemed to have been considered to take Charles' role.

He thought them through in the order that he had met
them the previous evening.

Leslie Blatt was the first. The repellent old playwright
had offered himself for the job and reckoned he was going
to do it, until told otherwise by Rick Harmer.

Rick had officiously taken over, even getting dressed and
made up for the part, before giving way to Charles himself.

And then Tony Wensleigh had forbidden Charles to go on
and said that he would go into the cupboard.

Leslie, Rick and Tony—each one of these at one time
thought—and no doubt told others—that he was going on
for Charles Paris. The pivotal issue then became: who had
each of them told? Or, who did the potential murderer think
he, or she, was stabbing?

Again Charles thought back. When he had met Nella
Lewis on the stairs, she had been coming down from the
floor where both Leslie Blatt and Rick Harmer were. And
she had told Charles that his part was going to be taken by
"that bastard." Since the two young A.S.M.s appeared to
have a harmonious relationship, it was reasonable to assume
that she referred to the old playwright. And since she was
then occupied for the rest of the Act "on the book," she
could well have continued to think that Leslie Blatt was the
occupant of the cupboard. And it might not be out of

character for her to respond violently to some septuagenarian assault on her virtue (an action that would certainly be in character for the playwright).

What was more, Nella had actually been carrying the dueling sword when Charles met her.

But no jumping to conclusions. On to the next potential victim.

Rick Harmer had put a lot of backs up in the company by his cockiness and success, but the only person he had roused to real anger was Leslie Blatt. The younger man's taunts obviously got through to the raw nerves of the older. Leslie Blatt had certainly been under the impression that Charles' part was to be taken by "young Mr. Smartypants." On top of that, he had intended to spend the Act backstage, which would have given him ample opportunity to choose his moment for a murderous stab through the canvas.

Then on to Antony Wensleigh. Who had arrived late on the scene, heard about Charles' condition from Rick Harmer, and announced the apparently firm decision that he was going to take over as Sir Reginald De Meaux (deceased).

Well, as Charles had just confirmed by the overheard telephone conversation, there was one person with a very substantial grudge against the Artistic Director. Rick Harmer was a very ambitious young man and Tony Wensleigh stood in the way of one of his ambitions.

It was like a game. Three sets of potential murderers and potential victims. And, in spite of all those permutations, the person who nearly got spitted was Charles Paris.

If he'd been standing up in his normal position when the lunge was made . . . The thought still gave him a nasty little frisson.

Drunkenness, he thought as he rose to buy himself another pint, does have its advantages.

CHAPTER
<u>FIVE</u>

THE MESSAGE IS MURDER moved into the second week of its run at the Regent Theatre, Rugland Spa, without further mishap. It was playing to over fifty per cent capacity, which was deemed to be very good business. Herbie Inchbald's words about anything "with 'murder' in the title" seemed to be being proved true. And the play was greeted with a few oohs and aahs and the modest applause which, regulars assured Charles, was the nearest the Rugland Spa audience got to enthusiasm.

Company life continued with its customary uneasy bickering. Kathy Kitson threw a tantrum one evening because the cold tap in her dressing room was dripping. Laurie Tichbourne caught a slight cold, which he treated as if it were an outbreak of cholera, and Nella Lewis ministered to him with hot lemon drinks and clean handkerchiefs. Rick Harmer hinted that his agent (that was his *acting* agent, of course, not his *literary* one) was having extremely interested inquiries about him for a major role in a major television series. Gay Milner insisted on lending everyone books about International Socialism, and Cherry Robson shrewdly started sleeping with a very rich local factory-owner. At meals after the show in The Happy Friend Chinese Restaurant and

Takeaway the Variety of Mr. Pang's Ice Creams remained fixed at Vanilla.

Life, in other words, was normal.

And Charles Paris had nothing to do.

The ways that actors spend their time when they're working in the provinces are various. Some spend it acting. Particularly in repertory companies, many of the cast of the evening's show will pass much of their day rehearsing the next production. Though tighter Equity regulations have prevented the hours of work that used to be expected, this can still agreeably occupy most of the day.

But Charles Paris wasn't in the next production, the much-debated *Shove It*, and was so deprived not only of occupation but also the social life of rehearsal.

Some actors, though not actually rehearsing, can still spend the entire day preparing for their evening's performance. The deeply serious tune themselves like precision instruments, working through relaxation exercises, preparatory walks and concentration games. The deeply lazy, like Laurie Tichbourne, can quite easily pass a day doing absolutely nothing. He would rise around eleven to a large breakfast, cooked by a loving landlady (he, needless to say, always ended up with a "treasure"), take a leisurely bath until lunch, eaten either at his digs or somewhere within strolling distance in the town, while away the afternoon perhaps with another sleep, then arrive at the theatre at seven o'clock complaining how tired he felt.

Charles Paris couldn't follow either of these courses. Even an actor marinated for a lifetime in Stanislavskian lore (which he certainly was not) would have had difficulty in "thinking himself into" the role of the defunct Sir Reginald De Meaux. And the Laurie Tichbourne method didn't work either. Charles was one of those people for whom stasis meant depression; to sit around all day was simply to offer an open invitation to all his worst thoughts. And since what he could only regard as the "loss" of Frances, those thoughts were even less welcome than usual.

Some actors, marooned in the provinces, are organized about their careers. They write lots of letters, to other

theatres, managements, television producers, casting directors, anyone who might lead to another job. They ring their
agents and other contacts, finding out what new shows are
coming up. They work hard, and are occasionally rewarded.

Charles Paris had long since ceased to believe that his
career would be affected by anything but the randomness of
fate.

Some actors, who have the ability, use the time to write,
trying out ideas, getting new shows together, trying to
interest managements in their wares.

Charles Paris, who had the ability, seemed to have lost the
desire to write.

Some actors take advantage of their environment. They
join the National Trust, they spend their days visiting stately
homes and other places of local interest.

Charles Paris never got round to doing that sort of thing.

Some actors pursue their sideline. It's amazing how many
extra talents actors have. Some are solicitors and do a little
gentle conveyancing for their colleagues. Some are doctors
and fit in the odd locum clinic. Some are collectors and use
their time with profit scouring the antique shops or bookshops
of the area.

Charles Paris had no sideline.

Of course, all actors go to the cinema in the afternoon.

Charles Paris did that.

But Rugland Spa only had two cinemas. And that left a
lot of the week unfilled.

The *Rugland Spa Gazette & Observer* was in the newsa-
gents on Thursday mornings, but Gordon Tremlett, who
knew everyone and how to get everything in the town, came
into his dressing room with a copy on the Wednesday
evening.

It was just after seven o'clock. Charles Paris, now *very
good* about being in for the "half," sat there meekly, his Sir
Reginald De Meaux gear complete but for the screw-on
sword and a fresh splash of Kensington Gore.

"Well, love, we're all over the local rag!"

Charles wondered whether Gordon Tremlett, in his previous existence, had addressed those groveling for overdrafts as "love." It seemed unlikely. No doubt such flamboyance was reserved for his wild evenings amongst the Rugland Spa Players.

"What do you mean?"

"The *Shove It* scandal, sweetie. Look, front page news."

The headline read "COUNCILLOR DENOUNCES 'SMUTTY' PLAY."

Charles shrugged. "They say all publicity's good publicity."

"Not sure in this case, love. Councillor Davenport's asking for an inquiry into the running of the Regent."

"Oh."

"He's not going to get it, of course. Herbie Inchbald slapped him down firmly at last night's council meeting. But I think it could all blow up into a rather nasty row. You seen the Mrs. Feller Brigade outside the front?"

Charles nodded. As he passed the theatre that afternoon he'd noticed a cluster of aggrieved ladies' hats and banners exhorting the public to "KEEP OUR THEATRE CLEAN," "BAN PORNOGRAPHY" and allow "NO OBSCENE SHOWS IN RUGLAND SPA."

"But surely that's the sort of publicity the show needs. Nothing like a bit of a controversy to fill the seats."

"Not here, dear."

"People'll come along just to see what the fuss is about. Broaden their minds."

"Oh no, love. People move to Rugland Spa *specifically* to have their minds narrowed. No, they'll stay away in droves."

"Are you sure?"

"Positive. Seen it before. No, this is a pity for the theatre. There are a lot of people in this town who'd like to get rid of the Regent. A lot of people on the council, unfortunately. Councillor Davenport and his lot want it sold. It's a prime site—any developer who got hold of it'd knock the theatre down and make a mint."

"But isn't the theatre a protected building?"

Gordon Tremlett shook his head wryly. "Not old enough or architecturally interesting enough to be listed. It is protected in a way, but the council could reverse that whenever they wanted to.''

"Why does this Davenport bloke want to get rid of it?''

"Wants the money to build a Leisure Center on the Leominster Road. His pet project. Always saying theatre's a waste of time; we should be investing in the health of the body rather than that of the mind.''

"Blimey.''

"Trouble is . . .'' Gordon tapped the paper. "Something like this doesn't do his cause any harm.'' The former bank manager pondered for a moment. "I wonder if all this has anything to do with what Donald was asking me . . .''

"What was that?''

"Oh, just wanted to pick my brains, share a little of my expertise . . .'' Gordon looked up mischievously. "You're not going to believe this, Charles, but I haven't always been an actor.''

Play along with him. "No. Really, Gordon?''

"No.'' With a complacent shake of his head. "No. And I don't think you'd ever guess what I used to be . . .''

Oh God, here we go. The worst-kept secret in Rugland Spa. "Why, what were you, Gordon?''

"Only a bank manager.''

"Good heavens.'' And, in case that was insufficient amazement, Charles added, "Well, well, what a turn-up.''

"Oh yes.'' Gordon smiled like the sphinx unburdened of her riddle.

"But what was Donald asking you then?''

"Ah well, you see, love, during my wicked past . . .'' Gordon chuckled at his wit, "I developed a certain familiarity with figures, account books, what-have-you . . .''

"Not surprising.''

"No. Anyway, I gather Donald's found some inconsistency in the theatre's books, don't know what, but he asked if I wouldn't mind casting an eye over them when I've got a moment. I don't think he wants to bring the accountants in and make it official. It's probably nothing, but I was wondering whether this threat of an inquiry's made him a bit nervous.''

"Could be."

"Yes." Gordon Tremlett rubbed his hands with glee. "Still, before I get on my slap and cossy to tread the boards . . ." (he always used far more theatrical slang than a real actor would) "I will cheer myself up with a nice notice. Frank Walby's column—always on the Entertainments Page, always on page fourteen, always restorative to the poor thespian ego."

He turned with relish to page fourteen, but the sudden change of his expression was enough to make Charles lean forward and read over the shoulder:

DATED THRILLER FAILS TO THRILL

Every cliché of the whodunit is present in the Regent's latest offering, THE MESSAGE IS MURDER by Leslie Blatt. Though the play had a modest success when it was first written in the fifties, post-SLEUTH and DEATHTRAP audiences require more sophistication in their thrills than this awkward little piece now has to offer. Throughout the evening disbelief is suspended so often that eventually one doesn't give a damn what happens next and only prays for a premature curtain to put the play out of its misery.

Nor are the show's chances improved by an untidy production by Antony Wensleigh. When the curtain rises on Hermione Halliwell's set, we suspect we are in for an evening of dated shabbiness, and nothing that happens subsequently dispels this impression.

The cast suffer the disadvantage of playing characters with no vestige of psychological credibility, but that doesn't excuse the display of hamming and fluffing to which we are treated. Kathy Kitson moves through her part like a shopwalker from Harrods and Laurie Tichbourne, as her son, is so wet you want to get up on stage and wring him out. Cherry Robson, as the maid Wilhelmina, sensibly makes no attempt to act and confines herself to looking pretty, while Gay Milner, an unlikely debutante, plays her part as if suffering from internal injury. Gordon Tremlett, impersonating a Colonel, gives a performance so unconvincing that it would not be tolerated by any amateur dramatic society in the country. The actor who emerges with most credit is Charles Paris, who is at least meant to˙ behave like a dead body, and who has least opportunity to do anything wrong.

All in all, THE MESSAGE IS MURDER is a production to be forgotten as soon as possible, and one that raises disturbing questions about the Regent's methods of play selection and overall artistic standards.

"Good God!" Gordon Tremlett exhaled in a shocked whisper. "He must have gone off his rocker."

"What?" asked Charles, who was just working out that "The actor who emerges with most credit is Charles Paris" was, if one forgot the rest of the sentence, a very quotable review.

"Well, I mean, Frank. He's had a brainstorm. He's gone, completely. He's never written like this about any other production."

"Perhaps he's never thought any other production was as bad."

"No, but I mean, some of the things he says here . . . I mean. Okay, it's a rubbishy old play—I was saying so to Leslie Blatt only the other day—but a critic should be able to look beyond the play. To say that I give a performance that wouldn't be tolerated in any amateur dramatic society in the country. . . I mean, those aren't the words of a sane man. Are they?"

"Well," said Charles judiciously, "it does seem a bit over the top."

"Over the top? It's nothing short of lunatic. And so hurtful." Gordon Tremlett slumped dramatically back in his chair. "I don't think critics realize how fragile an artist's confidence is. We have to go out there and give of ourselves every night, build ourselves up, bolster ourselves. And then, to be confronted with something like this. It's very puncturing to the ego."

Charles grimaced, recalling past punctures to his own ego. The bad reviews always stayed fixed, word for word, in his mind. Like the one from the *Aberdeen Evening Express*:

"With Charles Paris playing Dracula, dawn couldn't come soon enough for me."

Or the *Yorkshire Post*'s comment:

"Charles Paris kept hitching up his Northern accent like a loose bra-strap."

But perhaps the most wounding of all had been *Plays & Players'* reaction to his performance in one of the great classical roles:

"Charles Paris' Henry V had me rooting for the French at Agincourt."

ACT TWO

CHAPTER
<u>SIX</u>

"No, THERE's no doubt about it," Professor Weintraub announced. "Sir Reginald had been dead for at least eight hours when his body was discovered."

(On the Wednesday night of the second week that was true. Charles Paris had been an exemplary cadaver and was now sitting quietly in his dressing room reading.)

"But I don't see how that could be true," Felicity Kershaw objected. "I heard him talking on the telephone in the study just before we went out to play tennis."

"Yes, so did I," her fiancé agreed, trying desperately not to sound wet, "but we were fooled. That was just another part of the murderer's devilish plan. Look!"

Dramatically, he produced a spool of recording tape from his pocket. "Father had just bought one of those new-fangled tape recorders, and someone had set it in motion. So when we heard his voice, he was already dead!"

"How horrible," exclaimed Felicity Kershaw, starting to clutch at her stomach and then, not wishing to look as if she had an internal injury, stopping the gesture half-way.

"Oh yes, it is horrible," intoned Miss Laycock-Manderley, feeling extremely grateful that the *Rugland Spa Gazette & Observer* had not deemed her performance worthy of comment. "There is evil in the air at Wrothley Grange. I fear Sir Reginald's death may not be the last disaster we have to face before the day is out. I have a strange tingling in my spine."

"Now don't let's get things out of proportion," argued Lady Hilda, who wore a black silk dress for Act Two. This had been a source of some disagreement during rehearsal. Kathy Kitson had insisted that Lady Hilda De Meaux was the sort of woman who would instantly change into black after her husband's death. Tony Wensleigh, thinking of his Wardrobe budget, had felt this was unlikely, but, not for the first time in his life, had allowed himself to be swayed. However, when she had also announced that Lady Hilda was the sort of woman who would change into yet another silk dress (this time, she fancied, a pearl gray) for the dénouements of Act Three, he had said he really would have to put his foot down.

"Everything," Lady Hilda continued, "will be all right once the police arrive." With an elegant flick of her arm she looked at her watch. "I'm surprised they're not here yet. James, when you spoke to the station, did they say how long they would be?"

"About half an hour," James De Meaux replied as drily as he could.

"Hmm. And that was two hours ago."

"Ahah," Professor Weintraub joked inappropriately. "The good old English bobby, traveling as usual on his bicycle, yes?"

"You're sure they said half an hour, James?"

"Oh yes, mater," her son replied, because that was how Leslie Blatt thought the upper classes spoke. "The woman who answered said half an hour at the longest."

"Woman?"

"Yes."

"And you rang the station in Winklesham?"

"Yes, mater."

"But there aren't any women at that station. There's just Inspector Carruthers, Sergeant McIntosh and the two constables."

"What on earth does that mean, mater?"

"Oh, there's something horrible going on," Felicity Kershaw panted, again restraining herself from clutching at her vitals.

"Now let's keep calm. We'll ring the police again. Professor Weintraub, would you oblige?"

"Of course, milady."

"Ask the operator for 253."

"Yes, milady." The Professor jiggled the buttons of the telephone. "I am not seeming to be able to raise the operator. Ah no, somebody answers. Could I have, please, number 253? What? Who is this? Wilhelmina?"

Lady Hilda moved sharply across to him. "Let me take it. Wilhelmina? What are you doing? Where are you? Oh. Well, will you please come here straight away?" She put the phone down.

"Wilhelmina?" emoted Felicity Kershaw, her hand going involuntarily to her stomach. "You mean she planned it all? She murdered Sir Reginald?"

"No. She was in the study dusting when the telephone rang and she answered it."

"But how on the earth . . . ?" began Professor Weintraub.

"The telephone in the study is just an extension of this one. Someone has tampered with the machinery, so that when you ring from here, it can be answered from the study."

"So I didn't speak to the police station at all?"

"No, James. You spoke to someone in this house."

"Good heavens!"

"A woman. Did you recognize the voice?"

"Well, no. It was a very bad line. The voice was very muffled."

"A handkerchief over the receiver," Professor Weintraub announced. "This is an old ploy amongst the criminal fraternity."

James De Meaux looked menacing. "How do you know that, Professor?"

"Well, I, er . . ."

But he was spared further confusion by the entry of Wilhelmina, who stood in the doorway, looking pretty. She had decided that this was probably her role in life after all. She was very tired, after a few late nights at clubs in

Birmingham with her factory-owner. And since he, who was
separated from his wife and didn't seem to know what to do
with his money, had offered to take her on a trip to the West
Indies, she couldn't wait for the end of the run. See how
things sorted out. Maybe give up this acting lark.

"Yes, milady?"

"Wilhelmina, you just answered the phone in the study."

"Yes, milady."

"And spoke to us in here."

"Yes, milady."

"Has that ever happened before?"

"No, milady."

"Are you sure?"

"Certain, milady."

"Hmm. Now when James thought he was speaking to the
police, in fact he was speaking to someone in this house. A
woman." (Leslie Blatt's constant repetitions showed he had
no very high opinion of the retentive qualities of his audience's minds.) "Who was with you in here when you
telephoned, James?"

"Nobody, mater. I was alone." (This was true, as the
audience could bear witness. Act Two had started with the
relevant telephone call.)

"So it could have been anyone. James, you had better get
into the car and drive to Winklesham to fetch the police."

"Yes, mater."

"We have no other means of communication since the
telephone is not working."

At this moment (one of Leslie Blatt's personal favorites in
the play) the telephone rang. The entire cast froze, looking
at the instrument.

Wilhelmina was the first to move towards it, but was
stopped by her mistress. "No, I will answer it." Lady Hilda
raised the receiver. "Hello, Wrothley Grange. Ah, Laurence.
Where are you? Well, will you come to the Grange straight
away? What? Where? The bridge? What do you mean—
washed away? But—"

She looked at the receiver. "We have been cut off." She
looked at the assembled company. "That was Laurence.

The butler," she added, in case people had forgotten the earlier reference to him at the beginning of Act One. "He was calling from Winklesham. The bridge over the River Wink has been washed away by the freak high tide."

"Oh no!"

"But, mater, that means I can't drive to Winklesham to fetch the police."

"No, James. And I didn't have time to inform Laurence of Sir Reginald's death before we were cut off."

"No."

"Oh! That means we're all trapped here!" Felicity Kershaw had by now lost any inhibitions about her natural acting style and clutched her stomach enthusiastically.

"Yes. Trapped with Sir Reginald's murderer. Who must be one of us."

"Oh," moaned Miss Laycook-Manderley. "I knew there was evil in this house when I arrived. The deaths will not stop at one. The forces of evil demand their toll of blood."

"Don't go on so," reprimanded Lady Hilda (and most of the audience echoed the sentiment).

"No, we've got to be logical, think this through," said James.

"Yes. The person we are looking for is a woman with a knowledge of the workings of telephones," asserted Lady Hilda.

"Well, don't look at me. I'm an absolute rabbit at practical things. I can't even change a fuse." Felicity Kershaw went off into a peal of high-pitched laughter, deliberately excessive to point up the essential vacuity of the property-owning class which she represented.

"But why are we just looking for one person?" asked James, atypically incisive. "There might be a conspiracy. Suppose the woman who answered the telephone is in league with someone else, the one who actually tampered with the instruments. Maybe they planned the old man's murder between them."

There was a pause for the cast (and audience) to assimilate this new idea, before James continued, turning his best profile to the auditorium. "Professor, you brought a lot of recording equipment with you."

"Yes, but this is because of my bird-watching. I make records of bird-song. I am very anxious to capture the singing of the cormorant. This is why I bring it."

"But there are no cormorants round here. Not for miles," James countered.

"Ah, well, sorry, a mistake. When I say cormorant, I did not mean, er . . ."

"I don't think you'd recognize a cormorant if one flew in your face. Or any other bird, come to that. I don't think you brought your recording equipment and cameras for bird watching at all. I think you're more interested in the top-secret army research establishment in the pine forest."

"No, I—"

"I think you're a spy, Professor Weintraub. And I think my father recognized you as such. You may not know it, but my father was Head of British Intelligence during the last war!"

Professor Weintraub looked around the assembled company with panic in his eyes. "But I never knew this, I never knew it."

"I think my father invited you here to expose you, to show you up for the dirty little spy that you are!"

"No, it is not true!"

The ensuing pause was ended by Miss Laycock-Manderley with an utterance which, surprisingly and for the first time in the play, was not reminiscent of Cassandra. "If we're looking back to the last war," she said with a dryness that James De Meaux envied, "we might do worse than investigate Colonel Fripp's record."

"What do you mean?"

"He was in the Signals. One of the top boffins in Communications."

"Really?"

"Yes. Best known for his development of a new form of field telephone."

"Good heavens!"

"Where is Colonel Fripp?" Felicity Kershaw asked suddenly.

"I don't know," Lady Hilda replied with an elegant but

redundant gesture of a silk-clad arm. "I haven't seen him all afternoon."

"Nor have I."

"No, nor me."

"Wilhelmina, have you seen Colonel Fripp this afternoon?"

"Not since tea, milady. He said he wanted to take a good long look at the Titians in the Long Gallery."

"Oh. Well, would you see if he is still there, Wilhelmina?"

"Yes, milady."

Wilhelmina moved across to the double doors on the opposite side of the set from the fireplace.

Up in the front row of the Circle, Leslie Blatt's hand gripped the thigh of the fifteen-year-old he had picked up in the Wimpy Bar. "You'll enjoy this bit," he hissed. "Give you a real thrill."

Wilhelmina swung both doors open. Framed in them was the dangling figure of Colonel Fripp.

"Oh no!" screamed Lady Hilda, and then, perhaps thinking the play was on radio, "It's Colonel Fripp! He's hanged himself!"

At this point, to justify James De Meaux's next line, the body was meant to swing round with its back to the audience. But the body wasn't behaving at all in the way it had at rehearsal. It was twitching and struggling, but it didn't turn round.

James De Meaux said his line anyway. "Not hanged *himself*, mater. Not with his hands tied behind his back!"

Colonel Fripp continued to twitch and struggle as the curtain fell on Act Two. There was nothing amateur or unconvincing about the performance he was giving that night. He was giving the performance of his life.

Or perhaps, as the noose tightened around his neck, it would be more appropriate to say *for* his life.

CHAPTER
SEVEN

"THE TROUBLE WAS the rope was too short."

Nella Lewis seemed quite happy to go through the accident again for Charles, although she had presumably had to give her version to the police and other curious members of the company. She wasn't making a big production of it, just telling helpfully because he asked. She really was a very nice girl, he reflected. And astonishingly pretty. Wasted on Laurie Tichbourne.

But before any lecherous intent could form, the thought of Frances, like a trapped nerve, stopped him. Now that she was presumably off his scene, the thought of her was far more inhibiting to him than it had been when there was a real tie to feel guilty about.

"But he wasn't just being supported by the rope, was he, Nella?"

"Oh, no. Haven't you ever been hanged, Charles?"

"No. I've been decapitated once or twice, and had unspeakable things done to me in *Edward II*, but never actually been hanged."

"Well, it's like flying."

"Oh, I've done that. On the old Kirby wire."

"Yes. Well, for hanging you wear the same sort of

harness, you know, round the torso and under the crutch, and the wire clips on to the shackle in the same way. And the rope, the noose, is run up the wire into the flies.''

''Right.''

''Obviously the important thing is to get the relative tension between the rope and the wire right. It's got to be the wire that takes the strain, but you can't have the rope too slack or it sags and any illusion you might be creating is destroyed.''

''But for poor old Gordon it was the rope that took the strain?''

''Yes, with the wire slack. I don't know how it happened. It was a terrible accident.''

''Yes.'' If that was the right word. ''When did he get in position? Surely he didn't dangle there through the entire Act?''

''No. He'd get there about ten minutes before his appearance . . . I forget what the cue was exactly . . . but then either Rick or I would clip on the wire and arrange the noose for him.''

''But why didn't you notice there was something wrong then?''

''Ah, you see, he stood on a chair for that bit, so both the wire and the rope were slack. He only launched himself off on Kathy's line, 'Wilhelmina, have you seen Colonel Fripp this afternoon?' That was Tony's idea—he reckoned it was more effective if the body was swinging when the audience saw it.''

''So Gordon was only being throttled for a few minutes?''

''Yes, that's what saved his life—the fact that we were able to get him down so quickly. Mind you, he was lucky he didn't break his neck when he left the chair. I suppose the wire must have taken a bit of his weight.''

''Yes. And then the rope just slowly tightened up.''

''Right.''

''How is he? Have you heard?''

''Still in Intensive Care, I gather. Still touch and go.''

''Hmm.'' Two accidents now. A stabbing which caused no casualty, and a hanging which might have been accidental and which might yet prove fatal. Charles' mind struggled to detect a pattern to the sequence. And, with gloom worthy of Miss Laycock-Manderley, he wondered whether the sequence had ended or was going to get worse.

"And you've no idea how it happened?"

Nella shrugged. "Rick fixed the rope up in the flies. I suppose he could have misjudged the tension, but it's unlike him. He's pretty careful about most things."

"Yes." Rick Harmer, on the other hand, was one of the potential suspects for the stabbing, in the scenario that saw Antony Wensleigh as the intended victim. But the A.S.M. had a motive against the Director; and apparently none against the thespian bank manager.

"The only idea I've had," Nella offered hesitantly, "came from something Laurie said . . ."

"Yes?"

"Well, you saw that review in the *Gazette*?"

"Yes."

"It upset quite a few people."

"Everyone, I should think. Except me."

Nella smiled deliciously. "Well, Laurie was saying how upset Gordon had been about it, and I just wondered whether he . . . shortened the rope himself . . ."

"Gordon? Surely he wouldn't overreact that much. I mean, I know it upset him, but he's not a suicidal type."

"No, I didn't mean that. I mean that the review said he was unconvincing, and I wondered whether he said to himself, 'Unconvincing, huh? Well, I'll at least make sure the hanging looks convincing.' "

"And overdid it?"

"It's possible. It's the sort of daft, unprofessional thing he would do."

Charles jutted out his lower lip. "I suppose you could be right. Pretty violent, that review, wasn't it?"

"You can say that again."

"And, I gather, not typical."

"No. Total change of character. I think the booze must have got to him at last, rotted his brain away."

Then she blushed, remembering an earlier meeting with Charles and not wanting to think she was making comparisons. He smiled to ease the tension. "How did Laurie take it?"

She grimaced. "Not very well. I'm afraid he's a bit childish about that sort of thing. Threw a bit of a tantrum— said if that's what people thought of his performance, then he jolly well wasn't going to go on."

"But did, nonetheless."

"Yes, I managed to calm him down."

"Massaged his ego a little?"

She smiled again, slightly guiltily this time.

"Things all right between you and Laurie?"

"Yes," she asserted defensively. "Well, I mean, yes. He's very sweet, but . . . well, you know . . ."

"Yes, I know."

"He really seems to want a mother rather than a girl-friend."

"Yes. But you're quite gone on him?"

She nodded ruefully. "And he seems to be pleased about that, but just sort of to take it for granted . . ."

"Yes."

"I'm afraid it's not at the moment a very *dynamic* relationship."

"I don't think dynamics are Laurie's strong point."

"No. Oh well, it's the same old story. A—i.e., me— loves B, B isn't as keen as A is, and meanwhile A is hassled by the unwanted attentions of C."

But before the intriguing identity of C could be revealed, Rick Harmer came up. "Charles, Donald wants a word. Could you nip up to the office?"

"Sure. Continue our chat tomorrow, Nella?"

"Yes. Ooh no, I won't be here tomorrow. I've got to go to this All-Day Seminar thing in Worcester."

"Don't I know it," said Rick bitterly.

"What's this?"

Nella explained. "It's something for an Adult Education Institute, I think. A sort of Symposium on the theatre. Tony's going along to talk, and he's insisting on taking along a member of the Stage Management to answer questions on that side of it. God knows why he's chosen me—I'm fairly new to the business."

"He's chosen you," said Rick, "simply so that I'll be

needed here and won't be able to have the day free for the recording of my radio pilot."

"Oh. Do you really think so?"

"Yes, I do. Absolutely typical of him. Tony Wensleigh is a real bastard."

Once again Charles found it difficult to reconcile this description with what he knew of the Artistic Director.

Donald Mason was once again on the phone when Charles arrived in the administrative office. And once again he appeared to be sorting out some cock-up of Tony Wensleigh's.

"Look, I'm sorry to go through it again, but I would just like to check I've got my facts right, because, you know, if there has been any funny business . . . Yes, thank you. Right, you received the order for the Henry VIII costume on November 10th? Yes, that would tally, because round then we were thinking of organizing a series of medieval banquets in the bar, as a fund-raising exercise. But then we dropped the idea, and the order should have been cancelled. Yes, I remember distinctly reminding the Artistic Director to cancel. Are you sure he didn't? Hmm. You see, the thing that makes it awkward from my point of view is that when the costume did arrive, he then wore it to a fancy dress party on New Year's Eve. Yes, and then it was dispatched to you on January 2nd. No, no. I'm not blaming you in any way, I just want to get the facts right. You see, it could look—to an outsider—horribly as if he'd just ordered the costume for himself to wear to this party—and slapped the hire charge on to the theatre's account. So just in case anyone does start to make allegations like that, I have to know exactly what happened. Yes. I mean, I have to protect my Artistic Director. Right. Well, thank you very much indeed. You've been most helpful."

He put the phone down and, with a disarming smile, said, "Sorry, Charles. There's always something."

"Don't worry. You, er, wanted to see me." Once again Charles found himself feeling a bit Billy Bunterish.

"Yes." Donald Mason rose from his chair and moved

over to look out of the office's one small window. "Our last interview was on a rather unhappy subject . . ."

"Yes."

"Well, I think this one's going to be more cheerful. It's an ill wind and all that."

What on earth was he talking about?

"As you know, Charles, we had a rather nasty accident last night. Poor old Gordon . . . Incidentally, I've just been on to the hospital and the prognosis, you'll be glad to hear, sounds a little more hopeful. But the fact is, Gordon's going to be out of action for some time, whatever happens."

Oh. Was Charles about to be promoted from a stabbed corpse to a hanged corpse?

"Now Rick Harmer will be taking over from Gordon for the rest of the run of *The Message Is Murder*."

No, he wasn't.

"Rick's a very talented boy and can easily age up for the part. But the thing is that Gordon was also playing a small part in *Shove It* . . ."

So that was it. Charles' great talents were about to be enlisted in the service of Royston Everett's mucky writing.

"As I say, it's only a small part, but Rick can't play it, because you can't do that with make-up."

There was a slight pause before Charles asked, "Er, do *what* with make-up?"

"Well, you can manage a face easily, but you can't make the whole of a young body look like an old body."

"Ah. Do you mean this is a nude part?"

"Yes."

All right, all right, thought Charles. Now don't tell me that it's all absolutely necessary to the plot and will be very tastefully done.

"You'll be one of the prostitute's clients who are chased out when the police raid the flat."

"Oh. Great."

"There are a couple of lines. Nothing much. You just have to shout at the policemen."

"Oh yes." Charles could imagine the sort of thing he'd have to shout.

"I'd like you to do it, Charles—apart from anything else, to show there are no hard feelings about the other business. I have to tell you that Tony doesn't want you to have the part, because he thinks you're unreliable, but I'm prepared to overrule him on this occasion. That is, if you want to do it. It's another three weeks' work. What do you say? Will you do it—I mean, that is assuming that you're not going straight on to another job?"

No one who had been more familiar with Charles Paris' career would have asked the last question.

The letter had been directed on to the Regent Theatre by Charles' agent, Maurice Skellern. As soon as he recognized the writing, he felt a little welling of nauseous excitement in his throat. He didn't want to open it, but at the same time knew he had to.

Dear Charles,

I had hoped to hear from you after my last letter, but, since I haven't, there seemed nothing for it but to write again. I've tried ringing Hereford Road a few times, but when I finally got through, one of the Swedes said you were working, though she didn't know where. I somehow couldn't bring myself to ring Maurice, so I've sent this letter c/o him.

I do want to talk to you, Charles, now more than ever. Nothing has really changed since I last wrote, least of all my state of utter confusion. And though I know that seeing you would only confuse me more, I also know that you are probably the only person I can talk to.

I gather that you spoke to Juliet and have had horrors since that anything she said may have misled you, though I'm not quite clear what she did say and what would constitute misleading information.

Charles, we must not lose touch, now more than ever. Please ring me, or write to me—contact me somehow. I so want to talk to you.

I hope whatever you're doing is going well, wherever

you're doing it. And I hope you're more positively and
consistently happy than I am.
Love,
Frances

The letter threw him into a turmoil. Through his scrambled
emotions he could identify individually anger, jealousy, pity,
regret and even, infuriatingly, a little hope. Though hope for
what he was not sure.

The one clear point that emerged was that he should
phone Frances as soon as possible.

But, being Charles Paris, he put it off.

Shove It had been a *succès de scandale* of 1977. The
production, much-praised at the Liverpool Playhouse, had
transferred to the West End, where the critics, going through
one of their self-flagellating phases of gosh-we-must-stop-
watching-all-these-light-comedies-and-thrillers-and-really-
get-down-to-something-a-bit-searing-and-gritty, also praised
it extravagantly. With three changes of cast, it ran for two
and a half years, then did a national tour for another year,
until finally the rights were available for provincial theatres
to mount their own productions.

The play, a searingly accurate and unsentimental evoca-
tion of the tough area in which Royston Everett grew up,
made him enough money to settle in the South of France,
where he continued to make a great deal from writing
screenplays of films that never got made, and settled down
quietly to drink himself to death.

Nothing dates more quickly than yesterday's sensation,
and by the time it reached the Regent Theatre, Rugland Spa,
Shove It was more dated than the works of Thomas Shadwell
and Colley Cibber. Its power to shock had been weakened
by imitations on stage and television, the reliance of its
original success on a series of charismatic performances was
revealed, and all that remained was a rather shapeless piece,
full of long ranting monologues, with a lot of apparently
gratuitous bad language and nudity.

The performances that it was getting in Rugland Spa were

not charismatic. Nor did they seem to be in tune with the mood of the play.

Certainly Kathy Kitson wasn't. The first morning Charles arrived at rehearsal, she was already arguing with a very patient but pained-looking Tony Wensleigh.

"I'm sorry, Tony love, but I'm sure the madame of the brothel would wear a beige silk dress with blue flecks."

"I honestly think that's unlikely, Kathy. The play is set in a very depressed area and she's meant to be very poor."

"I know that, darling, but she's not the sort of woman who would let that sort of thing stop her from taking care of her appearance."

"But she couldn't afford a silk dress."

"Tony love, all the great courtesans of history have dressed magnificently, it's a well-known fact. I mean, Dubarry, Pompadour . . ."

"But she isn't Dubarry or Pompadour. She's a broken-down old whore, riddled with syphilis."

Kathy Kitson extended her long neck. "I don't think that sort of language is necessary, Tony."

"It's nothing to what's in the play."

"No. That's another thing I would like to have a long talk about."

"Yes, okay, Kathy. Later. We'd better get on with rehearsal now."

"I am quite ready to get on with rehearsal, Tony. I don't want to get sidetracked by all these discussions."

"No. Right. Fine. Let's take it from where the two punters come in and you offer the girls to them."

"Very well."

The cast for the scene got into their positions. Charles, who was playing one of the punters, was shown where to stand. He didn't have many actual lines in the scene, just a few lewd grunts and obscene reactions as the prostitutes were pointed out to him and a brief résumé of their special skills given by their keeper. (This scene had been hailed by *Time Out* as "a microcosm of English society, where the fat cats of plutocracy casually select which workers they intend to exploit." Gay

Milner, as one of the whores, was finding the part a lot easier to play politically than she did Felicity Kershaw.)

Tony Wensleigh clapped his hands, a gesture of authority which didn't suit him. "Okay, Kathy, you begin with 'If you're looking for a really good...' erm...etcetera..."

"Right you are, love."

The whores posed, according to their middle-class views of how whores might pose. The punters tried to look like lecherous old men (no great effort of character acting in at least one case). Kathy Kitson gave her eternally graceful impression of a shopwalker at Harrods.

"If you're looking for a really enjoyable evening," she elocuted, "perhaps one of these young ladies might prove a friendly companion for you. Sharon here has a great deal of charm—"

"Kathy, Kathy. Sorry, got to stop you."

"I was just getting into my flow, Tony."

"I know, I know. But those are not the lines in the script."

"You can't expect me to be word-perfect at this stage in rehearsal."

"That's not what I'm saying, Kathy. You are remarkably fluent for this stage in rehearsal. But what you are fluent in is not what Royston Everett wrote."

"He wrote that she offers the girls—I'm offering the girls." Kathy Kitson shrugged silk-clad shoulders.

"Yes, but he didn't write in the words that you used."

"I'm sure the audience will understand what I mean."

"I'm sure they will. But that's not the point. The author's lines matter. I mean, how would you feel if Hamlet came on for his big soliloquy and said, 'I can't decide whether to do myself in or not'?"

"This Everett person is hardly Shakespeare."

"No, I agree. But we are doing his play, that's what we are paying him royalties for, that's what the audience will come to the theatre expecting to see, and so that is the text that we should be presenting."

"I think what I am saying is much more tasteful."

"I don't question that, Kathy. But Royston Everett is not

trying to be tasteful. He is painting a picture of life as it really is, in the language which people really use."

"Oh, I don't think life is really like this. This is all so impossibly sordid. I mean, Tony love, is your life like this? Do you move amongst prostitutes all the time? I mean, when did you last meet a prostitute here in Rugland Spa? Go on, tell me."

"That is not—"

"Certainly, my life is nothing like this, I'm glad to say. My life's much more like a Noël Coward play than this sort of rubbish."

"Kathy, all I'm saying is that we should perform the play as written. I'm not saying that your life is like the life depicted here, but then you can't expect to be playing yourself all the time. You have to play other characters as well—that's what acting's about."

"Don't tell me what acting's about!"

"No, I'm sorry, I didn't mean that. I just mean that, okay, Royston Everett's language is not the sort of language you might use . . ."

"Certainly not."

"No. It's bold, and it's frank, and it's designed to shock. But we mustn't be pussy-footed about it. We must just say the words, not be ashamed of them. When the script says, 'If you're looking for a really good . . .' erm . . . , then we mustn't shy away from it. We must say the word, we must say, 'If you're looking for a really good . . .' erm . . . and so on . . . Okay, let's take it from the same place."

They continued the rehearsal. Seeing the play acted did not raise the opinion Charles had formed from reading it. The cast seemed to be lost in a morass of vituperation, and Tony Wensleigh showed no signs of being able to lead them out of it. He looked puzzled and was vaguer than ever. Scenes got plotted and intonations corrected, but he had no overall vision of the play. *Shove It* needed a strong directorial hand to camouflage its deficiencies, and it wasn't getting it. The cast needed the inspiration that could only be given by directorial enthusiasm, real or faked (theatre directors

have to rival prostitutes in faking enthusiasm). But Tony
Wensleigh seemed distracted, preoccupied, anxious even.

He certainly showed no aptitude for directing that sort of
play. He was workmanlike, the show would actually go on,
but it was alien to the director's nature. He excelled at the
subtleties of his craft, teasing performances out of small
casts, and was lost amidst the strident brashness of Royston
Everett's work.

Not for the first time, Charles wondered how the season's
play actually got selected. To choose one absolute stinker
might be regarded as a misfortune: to choose two in a row
looked like deliberate perversity.

That afternoon the cast was honored by a visit from Herbie
Inchbald. His entrance disrupted the rehearsal completely,
though for the first time in the day some kind of flow had
been established. With elaborate gestures and hushings he
explained that he didn't want to disrupt anything, just slip
into the back of the Drill Hall and watch a bit of the
rehearsal. They were to ignore him and just continue as if
he weren't there.

This was difficult. The presence of the Chairman of the
Theatre Board—particularly his unexplained presence—was
not easily ignored. But they did their best, and at least his
being there inhibited Kathy Kitson's meandering from the
text a little (though there were certain favorite words of
Royston Everett which she refused to utter).

After about ten minutes, the scene which they were
running came to an end, and Herbie Inchbald interrupted,
"Er, sorry, Tony, don't want to interrupt, but if I could just
say a couple of words . . ."

"Of course, Herbie."

"Erm, okay. If you could all gather round, team . . ."

Ugh. Charles didn't like people who called the company
"team." It seemed to him to fit in with people who called
the theatre the "thee-ettah."

"No, the reason I've come along today, team, is not
anything that need worry you. Fact is, you probably don't need
telling that this little show of yours is causing a bit of

controversy in Rugland Spa. Its reputation has gone before it and, let's face it, it's got a few of the local biddies a bit upset.

"Now this doesn't worry me. The history of the thee-ettah has been the history of ruffling public sensibilities— that's the only way new ideas get an airing, and the thee-ettah is a very important medium for spreading new ideas."

Gay Milner, slightly surprised at the source of this remark, still nodded agreement.

"No, it's my belief that, so long as what you're doing is artistically justified and is tastefully done, then it should be done. Our policy at the Regent—and particularly since Donald, our new General Manager, took over—has always been to provide varied fare. Okay, we do the standards, we do the panto, we do the Shakespeare, we do the Ayckbourn, we do a grand little thriller like *The Message Is Murder*. But we also have to be experimental—and that's why we're doing *Shove It*.

"You may wonder why I'm telling you all this. After all, you know it. But I wanted to come along in person and tell you that this little show has the full support of the Board— as well, of course, as that of the Artistic Director and General Manager. Don't worry about the opposition, don't worry about anything you read in the local paper. This is the sort of show the Regent ought to be doing."

Charles' respect for Herbie Inchbald rose. His arrival at rehearsal had been a good psychological move, to revive a doubting cast by assurances of management support. But he couldn't remove a niggling doubt about the artistic judgment of someone who liked *Shove It*, who could describe *The Message Is Murder* as "a grand little thriller" (and someone who pronounced theatre "thee-ettah").

Herbie Inchbald had not yet finished his team-talk. "You know, a few weeks back, I was talking to Michael Timson— you know, the M.P. . . ."

They knew. The name had been all over the newspapers three months earlier when he had resigned on an issue of principle over defense spending.

"We're members of the same club in London . . . Blake's . . ."

The name was dropped very casually, but still had the

desired effect of surprise. Blake's was one of the most exclusive clubs in the country. Obviously there was more to Herbie Inchbald than met the eye. He was, Charles had discovered, managing director of a local haulage company, fairly prosperous and socially acceptable in Rugland Spa, but not Charles' idea of a clubman. Still, the deceptiveness of appearances was a continuing source of amazement.

"And Michael and I got talking about his resignation, and, you know, he said something to me which I thought was very relevant to us here. He said, if you know you're right, do what you have to do, and all will turn out for the best."

Usual politician's vacuous rhetoric, thought Charles with reflex cynicism.

"So let's all have the courage of our convictions, eh? The Regent Thee-ettah has weathered a few storms in its time, and I'm sure it'll weather this one. It's been closed down, it's been bankrupt, it's nearly been brought up for development I don't know how many times. But it's always survived and it always will, so long as we stick to our policy of choosing the best plays and putting them on according to the highest artistic standards of the British thee-ettah."

Experience of many council meetings had taught Herbie Inchbald to bring a speech to a climax demanding applause (a device known in eighteenth-century theatre as a "claptrap"), and he didn't fail this time. The company clapped dutifully.

"Thank you. And just remember, the best you can do for me, and the rest of the Board, and for Donald, and Tony is to do this show so well that our critics and the Massed Wet Blankets of Rugland Spa haven't got a leg to stand on. Make *Shove It* an artistic landmark in the history of the Regent Thee-ettah!"

Again, he got his applause.

And Charles felt the same unease that he had on his earlier encounter with Herbie Inchbald.

The Chairman of the Board's enthusiasm for the theatre was unquestionable and admirable. But did he actually know anything about it?

CHAPTER
EIGHT

REGENT THEATRE "HANGING"—COUNCILLOR CONDEMNS
"NEGLIGENCE"—CALLS FOR INQUIRY.
by our Arts Correspondent, Frank Walby

The fortunes of Rugland Spa's beleaguered Regent Theatre suffered another setback last Wednesday with a near-fatal accident on stage to Gordon Tremlett, one of the theatre's regular actors (and former manager of Barclay's Bank in the High Street). A stage hanging in the Regent's current production, *The Message is Murder* by Leslie Blatt, turned out all too realistic for poor Gordon, who, in his own words, "found the noose tightening round my neck."

Speaking from his bed in the Chambers Kenton Hospital, where he is now recovering, the former Bank Manager is aware of how lucky an escape he had. "I don't remember much about it, but I gather I spent two days in Intensive Care and it was touch and go for a while." He paid tribute to the nursing skills of the doctors and nurses of the Chambers Kenton.

Gordon, who lives in Harfleur Avenue with his wife Anita and two children, Robert and Libby, and was a former star of the Rugland Spa Players before turning professional, says he won't let the accident deter him from continuing with his theatrical career. "As soon as I'm fit, I'll be back. When the right part comes up. If you've really got the theatre in your blood, it takes more than a hanging to get you off the boards. Just for the time being I'm resting, but I'll be back," he joked.

The incident, however, has a more serious side. Councillor Thomas Davenport, already severely critical of the running of the Regent Theatre, sees it as "just another in a long line of disasters caused by mismanagement and negligence. Obviously the equipment had not been checked properly." He complained that the theatre received a large grant from the Council, "which is just wasted money. Rugland Spa is not a wealthy town, and recent government spending cuts have put a serious strain on resources. Essential services like Meals on Wheels and pre-school playgroup facilities are having to be cut back, and there is a lamentable lack of sports facilities in the area. Maintaining the Council's grant to the Regent is just pouring good money after bad. An inquiry should be held into the running of the theatre."

(In recent years the Council has matched the grant made to the Regent by the Arts Council. But the Arts Council too is being forced to cut back, and the continuation of their grant is by no means certain. If that was withdrawn, the Council would be unlikely to find the full amount of the subsidy, and the theatre might be forced to close. This nearly happened five years ago, when the theatre was again threatened and nearly sold for development, but it was saved by a campaign of local people.)

Councillor Herbert Inchbald, answering Councillor Davenport's allegations, said Rugland Spa needed its theatre. As Chairman of the Theatre's Board, as well as a councillor, he felt a duty to provide this cultural amenity for the people of the area and not "give way to the forces of philistinism."

The theatre is also in the news at the moment, because of the controversy surrounding its next production, the outspoken West End success, *Shove It*, by Royston Everett, reputed to contain scenes of nudity and a great many four-letter words. Already opposition to the play is growing. Mrs.

Erica Feller, who is organizing the campaign against the production, says she is receiving "up to ten phone calls of support a day." She says the play, which she has not read, is "disgusting and representative of all that is worst in this country at the moment." Mrs. Feller, who lives in Ronston Gardens with her husband Norman and has won prizes for flower arrangement, led the successful campaign to stop the opening of a sex shop on Station Parade last year.

Councillor Inchbald said that the Regent Theatre has "nothing to be ashamed of," but announced that there would be a special meeting of the Theatre Board on Friday "to discuss ways of improving the Regent's public image, which has recently undergone a quite unnecessary battering."

Grapes were not really Charles' style, but they were more his style than flowers or chocolates, so he took grapes to the Chambers Kenton Hospital on the Wednesday afternoon of the third week of *The Message Is Murder*. (Wednesday was matinée day, which meant no afternoon rehearsal for *Shove It*, so Charles changed straight out of his costume after his appearance as the defunct Sir Reginald De Meaux. He thought the matinée audience could cope without seeing him at the curtain call. Actually, he doubted whether they'd notice; the average age at the matinée was even older than usual in Rugland Spa—in other words, about a hundred and fifty.)

The nurse told him he shouldn't stay long and tire the patient, but Gordon Tremlett looked indefatigable. He looked very fit and rosy in his room in the private wing. (Retired bank managers can afford health insurance schemes in a way that very few actors can.) He was surrounded by enough cards for a royal baby, enough flowers for the Guernsey Carnival and enough grapes, Charles noticed as he added his meager offering to the pile, to start producing his own Château Tremlett.

Gordon had recovered sufficiently from his shock to appreciate its dramatic possibilities and was more than ready to relive it for the benefit of any pair of willing ears. Most of the Rugland Spa Players had already been to pay their homage and listen to the action replay, so he was glad to see Charles as a new audience.

"It was my heart, you see, that's why I was so ill. The shock to the heart—would you believe, it actually stopped three times." He indicated the bandages round his neck dismissively. "Nasty rope-burn round here, you know, but that wasn't what did the damage. No, it was the old ticker, love. Touch and go, for a time, it was." He clearly enjoyed this phrase, because he repeated it. "Touch and go, you know, love."

"But you feel okay now?"

"Fit as the proverbial. Quacks say I'll have to take things a bit easy, but I'm sure once I get back on the green, Dr. Theatre'll sort me out."

Charles tried not to wince visibly at this barrage of theatrical slang. "And any idea how it happened?"

"Who can say, love? One of those things. One of the A.S.M.s got the tensions wrong, I suppose. They're not very experienced, those two. Need a few years before they're real *theatre* people."

"They always fixed it, did they?"

"Oh yes."

"I mean, you never went up into the flies yourself to check the ropes?"

Gordon Tremlett looked at him aghast. "Me, love? No! I have the most terrible head for heights—stand on a weighing machine and I get dizzy. No, no. Anyway, I can't be bothered with technical things when I'm on stage. Leave all that to the stage management. I'm always giving all my concentration to my performance."

Yes, ensuring that it's so unconvincing it wouldn't be tolerated in any amateur dramatic society in the country, Charles thought. That reminded him of the review, and of Frank Walby. "Have you seen this week's *Gazette*?"

This got a predictable actor's response. "And how, love! Not a bad little spread, eh?"

Obviously sheer quantity of coverage had erased the memory of Frank Walby's qualitative strictures. Still, the journalist had obviously interviewed Gordon for the front page article. Might be worth probing a little.

"Frank Walby wrote it, I see."

"Oh yes. Phoned through agog to talk to me, absolutely *agog*."

"Did you mention his review?"

Gordon Tremlett's face took on a saintly expression. "I think, Charles, something an actor has to learn..." He paused, and a note of reproof entered his voice, as if Charles had obscurely offended "...is magnanimity in the face of criticism. It is not for me to cast judgment on Frank's aberration, just to feel sorry for his circumstances." In an elaborate whisper, he added, "He *drinks*, you know."

So that was it. The review had now been dismissed as a symptom of alcoholic dementia. The punctures in Gordon Tremlett's ego had been repaired and it had been reinflated.

Charles allowed a silence to ensue. He knew exactly what he wanted to say next, but he wanted to present it with that what-on-earth-can-I-think-of-to-say-next desperation common to all hospital visits.

"It never occurred to you, I suppose, Gordon, that the hanging was anything other than an accident?"

"Charles! What on earth do you mean?"

"Well, the rope had always been the right length before. Why should it suddenly be wrong?"

"What, you mean someone was trying to *get at* me?"

Charles shrugged. "It's an idea."

"Yes, it is. How *thrilling*." Gordon seemed captivated by the suggestion, gleefully contemplating all of its dramatic possibilities. He no doubt had visions of inviting back all of the Rugland Spa Players to his bedside for sessions of intriguing speculation.

"You're suggesting, Charles, that someone might actually have *tampered* with the rope?"

"As I say, just an idea." Charles made it sound as much as possible as if he was suggesting a game of I-Spy or some other device to while away the afternoon.

"Yes, well, I suppose anyone could have gone up into the flies and *tampered*. It was all right for the matinée on

Wednesday, and there's never anyone in the theatre between the matinée and the evening show. Everyone rushes out to grab a drink or a bite to eat..."

"Right. So anyone who wanted to would have been pretty safe going up to the gallery and sabotaging the tackle."

"Yes. Oh, Charles, how *exciting*!"

"Very unlikely to have been seen doing it."

"You're right."

"The question is—who?

"Well, if they weren't seen, we've no way of knowing."

Gordon had obviously never gone through the mental processes involved in detective investigation.

"No, start from the other end. If anyone had been *seen* tampering with the rope, it would probably have come out by now. Instead, let's try and think who might *want* to tamper with the rope."

"Sorry, not with you, love."

Good God, how had someone as thick as this managed to run a bank?

"I mean—who might want you out of the way?"

"Oh, I *see*." The seriousness of the idea struck Gordon. "Oh, I'd never thought of it like that."

"No. Well, would you say you had any enemies in the company?"

"Oh, I don't think so. I mean, I'm just another actor, like the rest of you, you know, mucking in, sharing the knocks, the up and downs of theatre life, the camaraderie of the company..."

Dear oh dear. Soon he was going to burst into "Born In A Trunk," or produce a piano from under the bedclothes and say, "Let's do the show right here!"

"Okay, if you haven't got any enemies, do you perhaps know something about someone that he might want suppressed?"

"Sorry?"

"People do have secrets. You might have stumbled on something he'd rather have kept quiet."

"Oh, I'm with you. Well now, let me see." He looked

around with elaborate caution. "I know that Laurie and Nella are having an affair."

"Gordon, the whole company knows that."

"Do they?"

"Yes. Anything else?"

"Well..." Again the Official Secrets routine. "I have a strong suspicion that Kathy Kitson's hair is not naturally blond."

Charles sighed. This was uphill work. "That's hardly the sort of secret someone's going to commit murder to keep quiet."

"No, I suppose not."

This was all getting nowhere fast. Time to go.

"But there's no one else about whom you know anything discreditable?"

"I don't think so, no." Charles rose. "Well, except for Tony."

"Tony?"

"Well, perhaps this is telling tales out of school..."

"You can't stop there."

"No." Excitement at the drama of the situation quickly overcame Gordon Tremlett's scruples. "Well, I don't know if I'd mentioned this to you, love, and if I haven't, I think you may have difficulty in believing it—but before I came into the business I used to be a bank manager."

"No, Gordon. Really?"

"Oh yes. Here in Rugland Spa. And Tony had his account at my branch and... well, he wasn't very good at managing his money."

"What, anything criminal?"

"Oh no, love. Just incompetent. Always asking for over-drafts, you know, always hard up."

"Aren't we all?" said Charles, to keep the conversation light.

Gordon looked puzzled. "Are we?"

"Never mind. So Tony was always bad with money?"

"Terrible. With his own money, that is. He seemed to run the theatre all right, but his own affair were in a terrible mess."

"Did the theatre have its account at your bank too?"
"No."
So in fact Gordon Tremlett didn't know how Antony
Wensleigh ran the theatre's financial affairs. But he might
have been about to find out. Donald Mason had asked him
to look through the theatre's books to check some "inconsistency."

But Gordon Tremlett never got round to checking the
"inconsistency." Before he could do it, he was nearly killed
by an "accidental" hanging.

CHAPTER
<u>NINE</u>

A DISTURBING NUMBER of variables fitted into the new scenario. Casting Antony Wensleigh in the role of villain
explained a great deal which had hitherto been obscure. For
a start, it made sense of the Artistic Director's anxious air of
abstraction and his somnambulistic approach to the production of *Shove It*. If, as Charles was beginning to suspect,
Tony had had his hand in the till of the Regent for some
years, all the current demands for inquiries would naturally
be very disturbing for him. And the threat of investigation
by his former bank manager, who had no illusions about his
financial affairs, might lead the Artistic Director to extreme
measures.

Or maybe he had other reasons for wanting to silence
Gordon Tremlett. Maybe there was something else that an
investigation which questioned the actor might reveal. Charles
wondered. The odd thing about Gordon Tremlett's status
was how he had become a professional actor so late in life.
His talent was not so exceptional for anyone to make an
effort to secure his services, and yet he had got his full
Equity card. The only way he could have done that was to
be given one of the Regent Theatre's two provisional cards
granted annually, and after great competition, to two Acting

A.S.M.s, usually straight out of drama school. Why should Tony Wensleigh have awarded one of these prizes to Gordon? Previously Charles had just taken this as another example of the Artistic Director's bumbling bonhomie, based on his life-principle, "I like everyone to be happy." But this new suspicion put the incident in a more ominous light. Maybe Tony's magnanimity was in fact some sort of payment for services rendered. Had his bank manager showed especial liberality in the granting of overdrafts on the understanding that his way into the professional theatre would thus be eased?

If that were the case, it was not something that would do any credit to Tony Wensleigh if it came out in the course of an inquiry.

And it provided a further reason for silencing the former bank manager.

Another variable which slotted in with unappealing logic when Tony was cast as the villain was the attack on Charles himself. Hitherto his recollections of the evening of the stabbing had been lost in a blur of alcohol, but now the new concentration of his mind brought its events into sharp focus.

He recalled, with great accuracy, the whispered, persuading a skeptical Tony Wensleigh of his fitness to play Sir Reginald De Meaux. Charles remembered the excess of eloquence in which he had asked what threat was posed by "one slightly drunken middle-aged actor." It was not, he had said, as if he were about to expose the Artistic Director, denounce him to the Board, reveal a long history of fraud and peculation.

It had been random word-spinning, but to a man who actually had a long history of fraud and peculation, it must have sounded horribly pertinent and implied stores of knowledge of which Charles was innocent.

So Charles Paris, like Gordon Tremlett, had to be silenced. And only his drunken doze had made that silencing ineffective.

Charles shivered at the thought, because presumably he

still posed a threat to the increasingly paranoid Artistic
Director, and presumably there might be another attack.

He did not think that Tony Wensleigh was a deliberate
criminal, just a weak man who had slipped into an escala-
tion of crime. His first financial fiddling had probably arisen
out of incompetence, and then increased until he could not
manage without it. As its scale grew, so had his fear of
exposure, which had led him to the two attempted murders.
Like Watergate, the cover-up had been worse than the
original crime.

But unfortunately, the new scenario remained conjectural.
Charles had no hard evidence that Tony had been responsible for the two attacks. Nor did he even have evidence of
any of the financial misdemeanors.

But he had a feeling that Donald Mason might be building up a dossier on those. In spite of his occasional
assertions that he must support his colleague, the General
Manager was clearly having to spend too much of his time
dealing with Tony's administrative failures. The booking of
the rehearsal room was just an example of negligence, but
the incident of the hire of the Henry VIII costume was
potentially more serious. If Tony really had hired it for a
private function and slapped the charge on to the theatre's
account, that might be symptomatic of a general tendency to
regard the theatre's funds as his own private bank.

These petty malpractices might be overlooked in an Artistic Director of undoubted flair, but there now also seemed to
be big question marks over Tony Wensleigh's artistic judgment. Choosing a play as totally inappropriate to Rugland
Spa as *Shove It* was not an action likely to inspire confidence, and the way he was directing the piece was equally
disturbing.

If Tony was into wholesale fiddling, Charles wondered
for a moment why it hadn't come into the open earlier, but
decided that Donald Mason's arrival a year before had
stirred things. From all accounts, the previous General
Managers of the Regent has been lazier, less forceful individuals, no doubt content to let the Artistic Director run his

own company without too many questions as to how he was doing it.

Of course, Charles reflected, most of his suspicions against Tony arose from things he had heard from Donald Mason. But he felt inclined to believe them. His respect for the General Manager had risen considerably since their first meeting. Donald had shown such surprising humanity over his drunken lapse that Charles felt a debt of gratitude. Donald had also, in the face of opposition from Tony, offered Charles the new part in *Shove It*.

And he really did seem to care about the welfare of the Regent. Provincial theatres were very weak institutions and needed all the support they could get. It was a great bonus when someone of Donald Mason's undoubted administrative flair channelled his energies in their direction.

And if he had come to the theatre as General Manager to discover, presumably gradually, that the Artistic Director was not only lowering the artistic standards, but was also guilty of criminal malpractice, it must have put him in a very difficult position. The theatre was too exposed to survive a public scandal, and yet if its Artistic Director was a positive liability, some action would have to be taken.

And it would have to be taken before the Artistic Director took any further action himself. If Charles' conjecture was correct and Tony Wensleigh had deliberately tried to silence both him and Gordon Tremlett, then anyone else who knew anything to his discredit might also be under threat.

With Donald Mason as the most obvious next target.

Bad habits are quickly born, and on the Wednesday evening Charles decided that, his absence from the matinée curtain call having passed unremarked, nobody was very likely to notice whether or not he was there for the evening one. He therefore hastily shuffled off Sir Reginald De Meaux's mortal tweeds, and slipped out of the theatre towards the adjacent pub. He needed a quiet pint and a think.

There was a phone-box between the Stage Door and the pub door. He hesitated for a moment, contemplating ringing

Frances, but then decided he'd do that with more confidence after a drink.

Armed with the requisite pint, he moved into the corner of the bar. It was fairly empty, that sagging time of the evening when the drink-after-work crowd have reluctantly returned to their loved ones and the drink-before-bed crowd have not yet arrived. Act Two of *The Message Is Murder* was still unwinding its tortuous convolutions, so there were no refugees from the Regent. The pub was given over to the dedicated drinkers, and Rugland Spa was far too nice an area for there to be many of those.

The ones who were there seemed to be on their own, so there was little conversation, except for the girl and boy behind the bar discussing cavity wall insulation. Of the customers only one old lady talked. She was probably on her own too, though that didn't prevent her from directing her monologue to a crumpled figure who sat at the same table, with his back to Charles.

"You see, I know you," the old lady asserted, after a slurp of bottled Guinness. "Soon as you come in here I recognized your face. You come in here often, don't you?"

"Oh yes, an habitué of all the pubs," the slumped figure agreed. "Here, the George, the Railway Inn, the King's Arms, Hare and Hounds, you name it."

"Thought so." The old lady nodded her head complacently. "Never forget a face. I don't, never. Got one of those photographic memories, I have." She continued nodding, rather too long, in a way that left some doubt as to her mental fitness. "Your name's George, isn't it?"

The slumped figure was unable to agree with this.

"Oh well..." The old lady didn't seem put out by her error. "I knew a George once. Funny, he was. Used to wait outside the Convent and drop his trousers. Up the Angel, this was. You know Islington? Had a nice budgie, he did. Wanted me to take it when they took him to the Old People's. I said, no. I can't be doing with birds. All that cleaning out the cages, millet in your carpets... ooh, no. Not for me. Can you be doing with birds?"

"No." The man had reached the stage of drunkenness

when he would agree with anything. Perhaps he even regretted saying his name wasn't George. Anything for a quiet life.

"My daughter got a bird. Canary, hers is. Don't like that either. Not that I'd tell her. No, I'm grateful to her. She took me in when I had to move, didn't let me go to the Old People's. Not like George. So I wouldn't breathe a word against that bird, not in her presence. Might be hurtful." She took a contemplative swig of Guinness. "Still don't like it, though. Doesn't even talk. Can't see much point in having one that doesn't talk. I mean, there's no other point to them, is`there? You'd think if you got one that didn't talk, you'd take it back. You would if it was a washing machine," she concluded sagely and finished her Guinness. She held the glass up a long time, so that all the beige bubbles could drain down into her mouth.

Whether this was a deliberate hint, or whether he had just finished his own drink and felt full of alcoholic bonhomie, this prompted her companion to offer her another, which she simperingly accepted.

It was when he rose to get the drinks that Charles recognized the man as Frank Walby, theatre critic and arts correspondent of the *Rugland Spa Gazette & Observer*. He had the chipped plaster cherub look of Dylan Thomas. As Charles thought this, he realized that Walby's voice had the even lilt of Welsh in it. Local boy, probably. Rugland Spa was not that far from the Welsh border.

Charles drained his own pint and joined the critic at the bar, where the latter was trying to distract the staff from discussion of their heating bills.

"Frank Walby, isn't it?"

The arts correspondent agreed, without surprise, that it was. He had reached that stage of drunkenness when nothing seems incongruous, when the sudden appearance and conversation of strangers are part of a blurred natural sequence.

"I have to thank you for a very nice review in the *Gazette*."

"Eh?"

"For the show at the Regent."

"Oh." Frank Walby hiccoughed a laugh. "You can't mean the current production. No nice reviews there."

"Yes, I do. My name's Charles Paris."

"Oh." The memory of the name had been eroded by alcohol.

"The dead body," Charles prompted.

"Oh. Oh yes," Walby laughed again. "Rather back-handed compliment, though."

"But quotable."

"Yes. Must watch that. String together any two words that aren't downright abusive and some actor'll quote them."

Their drinks orders came and Charles paid for them, which again seemed quite natural to the critic. Nor did he find it odd that Charles followed him over to his table.

"Here, I know you," said the old lady.

"Oh, do you?" The words were out before Charles could stop them, a completely instinctive actor's reaction. What had she seen him in? Was she about to congratulate him on one of his rare television appearances?

"Your name's Lionel, isn't it?"

"No."

Again she was not deterred by the put-down. "Knew a Lionel once. Knew more than one, if the truth were out. One I knew best worked in the greengrocer. Had impetigo . . ."

She might have continued reminiscing in this vein for hours, had not Frank Walby suddenly sighed and announced, "I have immortal longings in me."

Whether or not the old lady recognized Cleopatra's words, they had the effect of silencing her, and she addressed herself to the thick head of her new Guinness.

"I know what you mean," said Charles.

"Sometimes," Frank Walby mused, "after a few drinks, the world seems very simple. Every ambition very easy, just hanging in front of me like a ripe fruit, ready for plucking . . ."

"Hmm," Charles agreed, playing along.

"And then, when I haven't had a few drinks, the fruit is snatched away from my lips like Tantalus, and every ambition seems insuperable." When he waxed poetic, he became more Welsh. "But now," he continued, with the elaborate logic of the drunk, "when I *have* had a few drinks, I can't imagine the times when I haven't had a few drinks, and I feel I can reach out and pluck . . ." He relished the word and repeated it ". . . pluck anything I want out of the sky."

"Ah, but a man's reach should exceed his grasp, or what's a heaven for?" Charles quoted.

"Good." Walby nodded enthusiastically. "Browning, good. You know, when I was young, I thought I was going to do everything. Thought it was all there, just waiting. Just waiting for the . . . plucking." Again he savored the word. "Fleet Street," he went on, with an expansive gesture, "the definitive novel . . . women—all waiting for me. Well, I did my bit on Fleet Street . . . eight months I did. Not all it's cracked up to be. And of course there've been women . . ."

"What about them?"

He shook his head carefully, as though afraid too violent a movement might dislodge it. "Not all they're cracked up to be either."

"And the definitive novel?"

"That . . . still remains to be done. Will be, will be," he hastened to assure Charles. "But I'm not quite ready yet. Still . . ." he hiccoughed. "Still gathering material."

"And meanwhile filling the time and paying the bills by doing theatre reviews for the *Rugland Spa Gazette & Observer*."

"Exactly." Another cautious nod. "Exactly." He somehow contrived to put too many Ts at the end of the word. "Just biding my time."

"And changing your style, I gather."

Charles hoped his probing was done with sufficient subtlety, but he needn't have worried. Frank Walby was drunk enough to be above suspicion.

"Changing my style, you're right. You see, until . . . until recently I didn't think the criticism mattered. I thought, don't stir it, keep everyone happy, they're all doing their best, give them the bene . . ." He took another assault on the word ". . . benefit of the doubt. But you can't go on like that. You see, time passes and, before I make my mark with the novel, why shouldn't I make my mark as a critic. Don't worry about people's reactions, the critic has a sacred duty to uphold absolute standards of excellence, and any falling off from those standards should be casti... casti..." He took a few runs at this one before managing to say "castigated."

"But why the sudden change of mind?"

"Snot a sudden change of mind. I've thought that all along. I've seen some unbelievably terrible shows at the Regent, unbelievably terrible. Every time I was writing my copy, I was working out all these really vicious things to say."

"Then why didn't you write them down?"

"Ah, well, as I say, didn't want to offend people. That's part of it. But also, not just that, I know a lot about the Regent Theatre. I mean, I've covered its ups and down ever since I've been on the paper—that's eleven years now..." The statistic seemed suddenly unfamiliar to him. "God, is it? Eleven years? Yes, it is. Eleven years. Must move on soon. Other things to be done. Where was I?"

"You've followed the ups and downs of the theatre..."

"Right. And it's been on the verge of closure so many times. Well, I don't want that to happen. You see, I do actually believe in the arts. I mean, when it says in the paper I'm arts correspondence—sorry, correspondent—it's not just the usual thing of someone being promoted from the gardening column or the sports pages. I do care about the arts, and I don't want the Regent to close. And God knows there are enough people in the town who do want it shut down—councillor and all—so I thought if I gave really strong reviews, I'd just be adding fuel to their fire. Look, they could say, not only does it cost a dispro...disprop ...disproportionate amount of money, it also puts on rubbishy productions—here, we've got press cuttings to prove it. I didn't want to give them that kind of ammunition. I mean, critics can be very powerful. Clive Barnes, you know, one of his notices could close a show on Broadway."

"I know."

"So I sort of held my fire, because I thought it would be

best for the theatre if I was bland and ano . . . adenoid . . .''
He gave up on ''anodyne'' . . . bland.''

''And what changed your mind?''

''Well, when I discovered that that wasn't all what the
theatre wanted, that I was weakening their cause rather than
helping it, that they were only going to be viable if they
were judged by the professional standards of West End
theatre, that harsh criticism would actually sharpen them up,
raise the quality of their productions.''

''What, someone actually said that to you?''

''Yes. He said that the Regent needed to be taken seriously as a theatre, not some kind of protected species. So I
should stop pulling my punches and start applying some
objective standards to the shows. He also said that that way
I would stand much more chance of making my mark as a
critic. So,'' Frank Walby concluded, ''I changed my style,
and you've seen the result in my notice for *The Message Is
Murder*. Much more trenchant, wouldn't you say?''

''Oh yes, certainly.'' The very word. ''Who was it who
suggested you make the change?''

''Donald Mason, the General Manager.''

Oh dear. One of Donald's ideas that hadn't come off.
Charles felt sure it had been done from the highest motives,
but he was equally sure it was a misjudgment. Notices like
Frank Walby's last one could only help Councillor Davenport's anti-theatre lobby.

Perhaps the General Manager hadn't been aware of the
pent-up stores of vituperation in the critic which his request
would unleash.

As if conjured, like the Devil, by the mention of his
name, Donald Mason appeared in the pub at this point. He
seemed to be looking for someone and, when his eyes lit on
Charles, appeared to have found his quarry.

''Sorry to interrupt you—oh, hello, Frank.''

''Evening, Donald.''

The old lady looked up from her Guinness and, stimulat-
ed by the new arrival, went into her routine. ''Here, I know
you.''

"I don't think so. Charles, do you think we could have a word?"

"Yes, of course."

"I do know you. From Islington days. Blenley Terrace, you come round to see me there."

"In private, if you don't mind, Charles . . ."

"Of course. Would you excuse us, Frank?"

"Be my guest." The critic made another lavish, but unfinished, gesture."

"Blenley Terrace it was, in 1972. Before I had to move out. I know your name, and all . . ."

The old lady was still maundering on as Charles and Donald left the bar. Frank Walby sat opposite her, smiling seraphically, as though listening to some virtuoso of the art of conversation.

To Charles' surprise, Donald didn't lead straight back to the theatre. Instead he indicated the stairs to the upper bar, which could not be seen from the one they had just left. "I don't often come in here, but I could use a drink. Don't know about you."

"Just had a couple, but I'll happily join you."

Charles had had enough fluid content from the beer and moved onto a large Bell's whisky. Donald Mason ordered a sugar-free lager.

When they had sat down, he said, "First, the official business. I'm afraid it's another reprimand."

"Oh dear. What, for sneaking out before the curtain call?"

Donald nodded ruefully. "Sorry, it sounds very petty, but I'm afraid you do have to be on your best behavior at the moment. As you've probably gathered, Tony didn't want you to stay and you're here on my say-so. And I've sort of vouched for your reliability."

"I'm sorry. It's unprofessional. Won't happen again."

"Normally it couldn't matter less. Most directors wouldn't insist on you being in the curtain call, anyway, with the part you have, but . . . I'm afraid Tony seems to be rather on his dignity these days."

"Yes."

"And I'm afraid he's out for anything he can get on me. So if you let us down, it's going to look as if it's my fault—or he'll certainly play up that side."

"I won't let you down."

"Sorry. As I say, just at the moment...Maybe the atmosphere will be a bit clearer after Friday."

"What's happening then?"

"This Extraordinary Board Meeting you may have read about."

"Ah yes. It's going to be a confrontation, is it?"

Donald shook his head sadly. "I'm afraid it may turn out that way. Not that I want that, but when someone starts making untrue allegations about you...well, you have to defend yourself."

"And even counter-attack."

"I hope that doesn't become necessary, but if it does, there are a few interesting points I could raise about Tony's management."

Charles could imagine what some of them were. He also felt, though he could not yet substantiate them, he could add some interesting allegations of his own, which might raise a few eyebrows among the Board members.

"So it's open warfare between the two of you now, is it?"

"I hope not, Charles, but it may come to that. The Board may have to choose between us."

"If they do, I should think you'd be all right. Herbie Inchbald seems to think very highly of you."

Donald grimaced modestly. "Has to. He backed me for the job and, I gather, overcame quite a bit of opposition to see I got it."

"And I'm sure he doesn't regret the decision. No, I'm afraid Tony's probably had things his own way for too long. Running the theatre for twelve years, obviously he's become a bit autocratic, doesn't like criticism, and seems rather to have lost his objective standards."

"Yes. Well, I'm certainly trying to remedy all that."

"By telling Frank Walby to write more savage reviews?" Charles asked with a smile.

The General Manager looked up sharply. "He told you that?"

"Yes. I know what you meant, but I think that idea rather backfired."

"Maybe. It's just the whole Regent set-up needs a few shocks to wake it out of its complacency. It has no cause to be complacent."

"No."

"The trouble is, Charles. Tony's so resistant to change, he fights everything every step of the way. Which is just so wasteful of time and energy. If we really worked together, I'm sure we could pick the theatre up out of this trough. As it is, we're just weakening it further. And if the divisions in the Regent's management become public . . . God knows, I do my best to present a united front, but it's not easy in the face of some of Tony's behavior. I sometimes wonder if he's quite sane."

"I think he may have lost touch with reality a bit."

"Hmm. That's a charitable way of putting it. But whatever it is, it's not helping the theatre one bit. The Regent is so fragile at the moment, so vulnerable. Wouldn't take much to topple it. If we lose our Arts Council grant, I can't see the Council coughing up the full subsidy. No, I reckon it would be dark within the month, sold and knocked down for development within the year."

"Wouldn't somebody step in to save it?"

"Don't know who." Donald Mason sighed. "Still, don't let's anticipate disaster. I gather you didn't do your curtain call this afternoon either."

"No. I'm sorry. I went to see Gordon."

"Yes, that's what Nella said. How did he seem?"

"Revoltingly healthy."

"Yes. Did he say anything interesting?"

"Like what?"

The General Manager looked at him shrewdly. "I'd never thought of you as a great friend of Gordon's, Charles. Nor the kind of person to rush round fulsomely to any invalid with crates of grapes.''

Charles found himself blushing. ''What do you mean?''

''Your reputation has preceded you, Charles.''

''Hmm?''

''A certain interest in detective work, a little mild investigation, a . . . what shall we say? . . . a nose for crime?''

''Ah.''

''I think that's why you went to see Gordon. I think you wondered to what extent his accident was accidental.''

Donald Mason was extremely shrewd. Charles paid him the compliment of telling him so.

''Thank you. And what conclusions did you form from talking to Gordon?''

Charles shrugged. ''Could have been an accident.''

''Yes?''

''On the other hand, the timing was odd . . .''

''In what way?''

''Because of what you had done that afternoon.''

Donald Mason flushed. ''What *I* had done that afternoon?''

''Yes. You'd asked Gordon to check through the theatre books for him.''

''Oh. That.''

''Yes. You'd asked him to check some 'inconsistency'.''

''Yes.''

''Was it some evidence of the books being fiddled?''

''I, er, don't think I should answer that.'' The awkwardness of the reply was as positive an affirmation as if he had actually said, ''Yes.''

''Fiddled by Tony?''

This time he would not even reply.

But his silence again spoke volumes.

And confirmed Charles' conjecture.

CHAPTER
<u>TEN</u>

CHARLES WOKE THE next morning feeling better than he had for some weeks. He also woke early, around seven o'clock, so he dressed quickly and left his digs before he could be subjected to more of Mimi's gloomy omniscience and another of her cremated breakfasts. He had woken up with a good intention and he wanted to realize it before it too got laid on the hardcore to hell.

He rang from a phone-box on the way to the station before eight. He knew she didn't get into the yellow Renault and drive to school till a quarter past.

Her voice, as she gave the number, sounded achingly familiar.

"Frances, it's me."

"Charles. Thank God you rang. I was beginning to worry that something had happened to you."

"Nothing more unusual than a job."

"Good. Where are you.?"

"Rugland Spa."

"My God. Knee-deep in retired Colonels and blue-rinsed widows."

"You have it in one."

"So no doubt the show you're doing for them is horribly genteel."

"No. By no means. I am participating in a thriller so bad I won't even mention its name, but I am also rehearsing for a play you may have heard of, called *Shove It*."

"Ah."

"Know it?"

"By reputation. Doesn't sound Rugland Spa fodder."

"It isn't. And let me tell you, this production features a significant first in British theater—a full-frontal Charles Paris."

"Oh, my God. When do you open?"

"Tuesday. Today we have our first Dr—... no, our first *Un*dress Rehearsal."

He paused. The initial impetus, the initial excitement of talking to her, had slowed down, and he felt very aware of the false brightness of their conversation. He also felt a sudden access of all the old mixed emotions, with jealousy well to the fore.

"Are you alone?" he asked suddenly.

"Yes." She sounded surprised. "Why, shouldn't I be?"

"Well, I thought your ... you know, this man ... this David. ..." Pretty inept. So much for the cool man-of-the-world *sang-froid* he had hoped to bring to the situation.

"No, of course he's not here. You've got the relationship all wrong."

Absurdly, he felt a gush of hope at her words. Maybe, after all, they were just friends. Or maybe no longer even friends ...

But her next words soon cast him down again. "We couldn't live together if we wanted to. David's married. Didn't I mention that?"

It was the familiarity with which she said the name that hurt.

"No. No. You didn't actually say ... just that there were complications. So ... the affair is illicit?"

"Yes. I suppose so." She giggled nervously. "I need to see you, Charles."

"Yes. I . . ." With an effort he held back from over-committing himself. "It'd be good to see you too."

"When are you through in Rugland Spa?"

"Not for a month."

"Oh, I must see you before that. Now we've actually made contact. I do need to talk to you. There's so much I want to say . . ."

But she didn't get the chance to say it. At that point the pips went.

And Charles didn't have any more change.

The turn-out for the first Undress Rehearsal of *Shove It* seemed unusually high. Perhaps, Charles reflected, there were no more members of the stage crew there than there would be for any other Dress Rehearsal in an outside rehearsal room, but he did wonder about the motives of some of those present. Certainly he couldn't think of any reason why Leslie Blatt should be there other than prurient interest.

There was about the proceedings an air of unnatural casualness. People joked too loudly to show how relaxed they were. Actors and actresses studied their crosswords and knitting with much greater concentration than they could usually muster. The ones who weren't going to have to take their clothes off seemed guilty and quite as unrelaxed as the rest of the company. (There were actually very few who didn't have to strip. Royston Everett's dramatic method seemed to involve every member of the dramatis personae baring their all at some point. *Time Out* had hailed this as "an important symbolic representation of the truism that men are born equal and free but are everywhere in the chains of class, convention and fascism.")

Charles felt quite as nervous as anyone else. He reckoned it must be worse for the men than the women. Female modesty was a traditionally powerful force, but, on the other hand, they didn't have the one great worry that dominated his mind (and, he wouldn't mind betting, the minds of most of the other male actors in the company).

That worry was extremely basic, and it dated back a long

time. It was a worry that had been present in changing-rooms at school, at Army medicals, and when wearing swimming trunks.

It was of course, What happens if I get an erection?

Though it was some years since Charles had worried about getting an erection at an inappropriate time (indeed, a more recent worry had been not getting one at an appropriate time), the anxiety had not diminished in intensity. The sense of shame involved was very primitive. (Presumably Adam's original recourse to the fig-leaf was born of some similar instinct.)

Charles tried to take his mind off psychosomatic stirrings in his underpants by concentrating on Tony Wensleigh. The revelations of the previous day made him see the Artistic Director in a completely different light, and his new disillusioned vision explained many inconsistencies of behavior.

It explained, first and foremost, Tony's air of manic anxiety. The director was surely the veteran of too many productions to be that worried about the show (it wasn't as if *he* had to take *his* clothes off, after all). Even a play as disastrously chosen as *Shove It* was the sort of thing an experienced director of three-weekly rep ought to be able to take in his stride.

But, if one interpreted his anxiety as that of a man facing total exposure of many years of mishandling theatre funds, of a man prepared to kill to keep his secret quiet, everything became clearer.

The same applied to his general air of abstraction and lack of concentration on the job in hand. There was only one important date on Tony Wensleigh's horizon and that was the moment the following evening when he had to face the Theatre Board and try to prevent his own fall by shooting down his General Manager.

Tony Wensleigh was a desperate man, prepared to do anything to save his position in the Regent Theatre.

In spite of the strained atmosphere of this-is-all-perfectly-normal-nothing-unusual, some concessions had been made to the modesty of the performers. Two sets of screens had been set up either side of the acting area "to represent the exits and entrances to the wings" (though tape markings on the floor had been thought sufficient at all previous rehearsals). The effect of this was to give a measure of surprise to each new entrance (as well as a measure of privacy to the shyer members of the cast.).

Behind the screens Charles Paris, who had the advantage of making his first entrance with clothes on, chatted with heavy unconcern to a young actor, who had thrown off all his garments immediately on arrival in the rehearsal room.

"You done, er, this sort of thing before?"

"Oh yes. Did a year in *O, Calcutta!*"

"Oh." The new generation of actors had a totally different training from his own, Charles reflected.

"And of course a good few movies."

"Ah. Yes. Of course." The young man seemed amiable enough. Charles decided he dared to confide his great anxiety. "Tell me, when you are doing that sort of work . . ."

"The movies, you mean?"

"Yes . . . do you ever have any trouble with . . . erections?"

"All the time, mate, all the time."

"Really?"

"Oh yes. I've tried everything, nothing has any effect."

"Oh dear."

"Total disaster. Whatever I do, I can't keep it up."

Ah, thought Charles, *that* sort of movie.

The opening scene of *Shove It* had been highly praised by the London critics. One of them, more pretentious and deluded than the rest, had found it in "parodic echoes of Restoration drama, producing by linguistic inversion a comment on the conventions of theatrical artifice." What he actually meant was that the scene had been lifted from *The Way of the World* and the language dirtied up in the approved Royston Everett manner.

The broken-down old whore and brothel-keeper, Sylv, like Congreve's Lady Wishfort, is, in the eighteenth-century phrase, "at her toilet." The maid, Foible, is represented in the modern version by the retarded teenage prostitute, Tracey.

But, whereas the audience only sees selected sections of Lady Wishfort's preparations to face the world, Sylv enters stark naked and goes through the whole process of dressing and painting.

Her first line is the repetition, five times, of a well-known four-letter word, which one Liverpool critic, intoxicated by the righteousness of the play's social comment, actually had the nerve to compare to King Lear's "Never, never, never, never, never."

In the Rugland Spa production to *Shove It*, the part of Sylv was being played by Kathy Kitson.

There was more than the usual anticipation at an outside Dress Rehearsal as the A.S.M.'s called for quiet and the Act One beginners crowded behind the screens. Tony Wensleigh, his large eyes glistening with anxiety, announced, "Okay, let's take it from the top. As straight through as we can make it. We'll only stop if there's some really major disaster."

There was silence. The acting space between the screens was empty.

Then Kathy Kitson entered.

She was dressed in a beige, silk ruffled negligée.

"Oh dear," she said, in her usual beautifully modulated but totally characterless voice. "Oh dear. Oh dear, Oh dear. Oh dear."

"Sorry. I've got to stop you there."

Kathy Kitson turned innocently to the Artistic Director. "You said you'd only stop for major disasters."

"Kathy, this *is* a major disaster. Look, you know you're meant to be making this entrance completely naked...?"

"Yes." She nodded confidently, as if she had given a complete answer to his question.

"Well, Kathy, I mean I hesitate to state the obvious, but I think it must be clear to everyone that you are not naked."

"Oh, is *that* it?" She spoke chidingly, as if he had picked her up on some minuscule detail of performance.

"Yes, that is it. Look, I'm sorry, Kathy, but we're beyond the moment for coyness. When you read the script and agreed to play the part, it was made quite clear to you that you would have to take your clothes off. I remember, we had long discussions with your agent about that very matter and got his full assurance of your agreement.''

Kathy Kitson stretched her neck loftily. ''Tony dear, when you book an experienced actress, you don't only book the actress, you also book the experience and the judgment that that experience brings. And my judgment is that this scene is more effective with me *acting* naked than actually *being* naked.''

''*Acting* naked?'' the director repeated weakly.

''Yes, darling. I knew you'd agree.'' Kathy Kitson moved back towards the screens with an air of triumph. ''Would you like me to make the entrance again?'' she asked with sweet humility.

''Kathy. . .'' Tony Wensleigh spoke with great weariness. ''That's not all.''

''Oh. Something else, love?''

''The line you spoke was not the line that Royston Everett wrote.''

The actress conceded that this was indeed the case. ''But my line does get over the same feeling as his. And so much more *tastefully,* don't you think?''

The rehearsal did proceed, after a fashion, though Kathy Kitson resolutely continued to wear her negligée. At the moment she was meant to put on her dress, she removed the garment to reveal a delightful silken petticoat.

She also resolutely continued to expurgate Royston Everett's lines.

And Tony Wensleigh, sunk in an apathetic gloom whose cause Charles felt confident he now knew, made no further attempt to stop her.

The rest of the cast who had to strip did so without demur. As garment after garment slipped off, revealing no greater excitement than the odd appendix scar and some surprising evidence of dyed hair, both female and male. Charles felt his main anxiety recede. Human flesh is not aphrodisiac under all circumstances, and in the goose-pimply chill of the Drill Hall, Rugland Spa, it had the opposite effect. Charles found his mind dwelling on butchers' shops rather than sex, and when his own turn came to reveal all, he hardly thought about what he was doing.

The only person who did seem to find the flesh on display exciting was the one person who shouldn't have been there, Leslie Blatt. Given the evidence he had already shown of a Peeping Tom mentality, it was no great surprise, but Charles did find it mildly revolting. The playwright was of a generation to whom permissiveness, if it came at all, had come late, and his reactions were those of a twelve-year-old sniggering over a dirty picture.

Charles felt glad for Nella Lewis's sake that she wasn't in *Shove It*, because she was so obviously the center of the old man's smutty desires. Laurie Tichbourne wasn't in the play either, so he was not around to protect her from unwanted attentions. On the other hand, Charles reflected, he couldn't actually see Laurie doing anything so positive, even if he had been there.

Nella was prompting, because at this stage of rehearsal the lines were still a little shaky, and, since no one could ever quite predict what cue they were going to get from Kathy Kitson, there were frequent breakdowns in the dialogue. The A.S.M. sat demurely on a chair behind one of the screens, her eyes fixed on the page, perhaps just in punctilious discharge of her duties or maybe out of modesty in the face of all that naked flesh.

Leslie Blatt hung around behind the same screen, alternately ogling other female members of the cast and passing comments to Nella. As Charles made his naked exit after the police raid on the brothel, he heard the old man breathe in the A.S.M.'s ear, "Pretty strong meat, this. Couldn't have written this sort of stuff in my day. Didn't know what I was missing, eh?" He sniggered adolescently. "Still, healthier times now. Healthier attitudes people've got. Very healthy, very nice to see all these naked bodies around, eh?" Then he leaned forward, pressing himself very close against the back of Nella's chair. "Though, of course, there are some one would rather see than others."

The girl's eyes did not leave the page, nor did any part of

her body move except her right arm. But that moved decisively, and the sharp point of its elbow was unerringly accurate.

"Mmmf," squeaked Leslie Blatt.

And "Good girl," thought Charles Paris, as the old man moved away from the chair, doubled up with pain.

The police raid ended Act One of *Shove It*. It was a kind of climax and, given Royston Everett's dramatic method, this meant that more people had their clothes off at that point than at any other in the course of the play (except for the end of Act Two). The last words before the interval were spoken by Sylv and were an exact repetition of the five with which she opened the play (a device which had prompted one of the sillier critics to speak of "an almost classical demonstration of cyclical unity").

The naked gathered behind the screens as Kathy Kitson moved to center stage (a habit she had) to deliver herself of the same—or who could say, perhaps some new—euphemism. But what she would have said at that rehearsal was never revealed.

Because at that moment came the Invasion of the Hats.

The doors of the Drill Hall burst open and, led by the redoubtable hat of Mrs. Feller, in marched the Massed Hats of Opposition to *Shove It*.

There were about a dozen of them. Most carried banners. To those with which they had picketed the theater had been added such choice slogans as "DON'T POISON THE MINDS OF OUR CHILDREN, "NO ROMANS IN BRITAIN HERE," "FILTH CORRUPTS" and, rather surprisingly, "YOU KNOW WHERE YOU CAN SHOVE IT!"

In the wake of the hats, shamefaced and wishing he was anywhere else in the world, was dragged a very young policeman.

The aim of the demonstration was disruption and the first action of the hats, loudly shouting out the slogans on their banners, was to knock down the two screens. The sheer size of the nudist colonies these revealed struck them dumb.

In the ensuing silence Tony Wensleigh's voice could be

heard weakly asking what on earth that thought they were doing.

"There!" Mrs. Feller pointed an accusatory finger, as far as Charles could see, directly at him, and turned to the young policeman saying, "If that isn't an obscene display, I'd like to know what is."

"Well, erm . . ." The wretched young man blushed beet-root. "In fact, the law on obscenity is not always clear . . ."

"But this is clearly obscene," insisted Mrs. Feller.

"Well, it might be, but, even if it were, I'm not quite sure what I could do about it."

"Not sure? I'll tell you exactly what you could do—and exactly what you should do—arrest the lot of them!"

The young policeman looked even unhappier. The prospect of rounding up a dozen naked men and women and marching them through the streets of Rugland Spa to the police station was not one that appealed to him.

He tried to look authoritative by getting out a notebook and pencil. "Right," he began tentatively. "Who's in charge here?"

"I am," Tony Wensleigh replied.

But not for long, thought Charles. This latest incident was just what the Artistic Director didn't need. Charles wouldn't have offered much for Tony Wensleigh's chances at the Extraordinary Board Meeting the following evening.

CHAPTER
<u>ELEVEN</u>

MRS. FELLER did not get any arrests, but she achieved the lesser objective of totally sabotaging the Undress Rehearsal. By the time the Hats had been cleared from the Drill Hall, the cast had all apologetically put their clothes back on again and it was too late to start on Act Two of Royston Everett's little masterpiece. Even if the cast of the evening's show had foregone the break due to them between rehearsal and performance, there wouldn't have been time. So a somewhat sheepish little group traipsed back to the Regent Theatre.

Where at least one of them was met with a further set-back. Charles, now feeling that he should watch the Artistic Director's every move, had walked back with him from the rehearsal room, but there had been little conversation. Tony Wensleigh was sunk in a gloom of his own.

But they were still walking together when they entered the foyer of the theatre, and so Charles overheard the words of Donald Mason, who rushed up anxiously to his colleague as if he had been awaiting his return for some time.

"Tony," the General Manager whispered, as Charles moved away, "just had a call from Nigel Hudson."

"Nigel Hudson?"

"My contact at the Arts Council."

"Oh yes."

"Well, it wasn't so much a call as a tip-off. Apparently our grant prospects are dicier than we thought."

"Oh."

"They're going to make their recommendations within the next fortnight."

"Oh yes?"

"And they're sending the assessment team down to the first night of *Shove It* to, as Nigel charmingly put it, 'give us a final chance'."

Which, Charles reflected as he left the foyer, was, considering the current state of the production, tantamount to a straight refusal of the grant.

But the new blow aroused very little reaction in the traumatized Artistic Director. All it got was another dulled "Oh yes?"

Charles was surprised to find there was a telegram for him backstage. There are perhaps actors whose lives are full of ecstatic messages from fans and urgent news from agents about film offers, but he wasn't one of them.

His first reaction was that something awful had happened to someone in the family. Juliet was ill. One of the grandchildren had been in a car accident.

It was family. But it wasn't bad news. Or, he decided quickly before his mind was swamped with mixed emotions, it probably wasn't bad news.

"COMING DOWN TO RUGLAND SPA FOR LUNCH ON SUNDAY. RING ME IF YOU CAN'T MAKE IT. LOVE. FRANCES."

The dear departed Sir Reginald De Meaux was now on his best behavior. He had given his word to Donald Mason and, not wishing to add to the dissension between General Manager and Artistic Director, he therefore did not even contemplate a visit to the pub after he had discharged his artistic duties in the Thursday night performance of *The Message Is Murder*. He would wait around for the curtain call, following Tony Wensleigh's desires.

Other nights he would have been content to sit quietly

with a book (he was rereading Samuel Butler's *Erewhon* and enjoying the experience), but on this occasion he felt twitchy and couldn't concentrate. His dressing room chair felt uncomfortable, and Leslie Blatt's banal dialogue, half-heard over the loudspeaker, was a constant distraction.

Partly, he knew, it was the telegram. The prospect of seeing Frances filled him with reactions he didn't want to itemize.

But there was also a general air of tension in the theatre. The afternoon's débâcle would normally have been laughed off by the company, but it merely added to the anxiety over *Shove It*. The show was due to open the following Wednesday and everyone was aware that it was well behind schedule. They were also becoming aware, given no assurances to the contrary from their director, that it was not a very good play.

The state of Regent's internal politics was also starting to have its effect on the company. The conflict between General Manager and Artistic Director could no longer be disguised. Nor could the importance, for the future of the theatre, of the following evening's Extraordinary Meeting of the Board. All this added pressure to the normal anxieties of a week before a new production opens.

For Charles, who reckoned he had deeper insight into the real causes of the divisions in the theatre, the stress was greater. He could recognize the increasing strains on Tony Wensleigh, feared that they might resolve themselves into violence, and yet felt impotent to stop the escalating sequence of crime.

If only he had some proof of Tony's involvement in the earlier attacks . . .

He decided to go up into the gallery and watch the Act Two hanging of Colonel Fripp (now being played with rather more conviction, because, in spite of his years, he had more talent than Gordon Tremlett, by Rick Harmer). Seeing the effect repeated might give Charles some clue as to exactly how the accident had been staged.

The top floor of the Regent Theatre was quite complex. The central area was the decorated ceiling of the auditorium with the roof directly above it. Above the stage was the flying space with a gallery on either side. In the front of the building, above the bar, was the space into which the administrative office was crammed.

But along the sides, joining the front of the theatre to the back, were two broad passages. The primary function of these was to give access to the catwalk round the auditorium from which much of the lighting was fixed, but because storage space is always at a premium in a repertory theatre, they were also used for other purposes. One side, on long mobile rails, was kept the company's stock of all-purpose costumes (the sort of peasant blouses and leather jerkins which would see service in anything from medieval mystery plays, through pantomime, to Robert Bolt). The other side was used as a prop store, where Roman helmets nestled side by side with papier-mâché marrows, rubber skulls dangling by strings of plastic onions, glass jewelry hung from deer's antlers, and tennis rackets poked from witches' cauldrons.

Both of the stores had doors at either end, giving access to the flying gallery and the administrative office area.

Charles had climbed up the wall-ladder to the gallery and was inspecting the counter-weighting of the wire from which Rick Harmer was about to be suspended when he heard a noise from the props store.

The door was closed. Charles had seen Nella, Rick and the other members of the Stage Management down at floor level. They were the only people who might have legitimate cause to go to the prop store during a performance. Alert to the danger of another act of sabotage, Charles decided that he should investigate.

He opened the door with extreme caution, but the light it admitted put the intruder on his guard. From the far side of the gloom a torch-beam swung round into Charles' face, blinding him.

"Charles." The voice, which he recognized, sounded relieved. Then Charles thought he heard a click, like the throwing of an electrical switch.

There was sufficient light from the door for him to see a light-switch on the wall nearby. He flicked it. Two naked hanging bulbs illuminated the scene. He stepped inside and closed the door.

Tony Wensleigh was momentarily thrown by the sudden light and froze. He was crouched in the far corner of the store by a fiberglass sundial and a pile of breastplates made of stiffened felt. In his hand he held a World War I army revolver.

After the shock he moved hastily, shuffling the breast plates back against the wall, tucking a dangling string behind a grandfather clock before he turned back to Charles with apparent insouciance.

"What on earth are you doing here?"

"Just heard a noise and wondered who it was."

"Oh."

The monosyllable seemed to require further explanation. "I was just going for a walk around the gallery, you know, killing time."

"Yes, of course. You do have a long wait between your appearance and the curtain call."

"Yes," Charles agreed, with some edge.

"Why do you do it?"

"What?"

"Why do you wait? Why not just get changed straight away? I'm sure no one notices whether you're there or not at the curtain call."

Charles looked at the Artistic Director in amazement. "I do it because you specifically asked me to."

"Oh, did I?" Tony looked confused, suddenly like an old man. "I'm sorry. I keep mixing things up. Do things and can't remember I've done them. Don't do things and think I have done them. Sorry." He rubbed his hand across his brow, as though his mental state were something external, that could be wiped away.

"You've been under a lot of pressure recently, Tony," said Charles gently.

The Artistic Director gave a weary smile. "That is a wonderful understatement. A lot of pressure, yes. I wonder how much pressure it takes before a man cracks. How many straws can a camel take cheerfully, and how does he recog-

nize the one that's going to do the damage? Does it carry a
Government Health Warning?''

He let out a bark of nervous laughter. Then silence came
between them. With surprising clarity further banalities by
Leslie Blatt filtered up from the stage.

Charles kept his therapist's tone of voice. "Tony, you
don't have to crack up completely. You can save yourself,
you can talk, tell the truth.''

"Yes, I firmly intend to. Get the truth out into the open,
then the pressure'll go away.''

"Exactly. And you'll feel a lot better.''

"Yes.'' The Artistic Director seemed calmer. "Yes, I'll get
people to listen to my side. Then they'll realize I'm not mad.''

"Of course they will,'' Charles soothed.

"And the nightmare'll soon be over.''

"Yes. You can put an end to it whenever you want to. It's
up to you.''

"You're right, Charles.'' The Artistic Director looked
directly into his eyes. "It's all a lot clearer now, what I
should do. I've been very confused the last few weeks, but
now it's coming clear.''

"Good.''

The revolver was still in Tony's hand. Charles thought the
atmosphere had relaxed sufficiently for him to mention it.

"Where did that come from, Tony?''

The Artistic Director looked down, as though noticing the
weapon for the first time. "Oh, that. I just found it up here.
Forgotten we'd got it. Came from one of my first productions at the Regent. *Journey's End.* In the early days we
didn't have any money. We could just afford the cast, but
nothing left for costumes and props . . . So we put out an
appeal in the *Gazette*—anyone got any First World War
uniforms and stuff they'd lend us. Quite a good response.
This came from an old girl who'd had two brothers in the
war. They'd both been wounded, and she'd nursed them
both until they died. She'd kept everything . . . all their
uniforms, everything . . . and she said we could borrow them
because of the play . . . because *Journey's End* was against

war, and she hated war. I don't know why we've still got this. We should have given it back . . . I can't remember . . ."

Once again the clouds of confusion were gathering. He pulled himself together with an effort. "The old lady gave us all the ammunition, too. She'd kept that." He gave a little laugh. "We shouldn't really have used a gun like this on stage. Not one that works. Should have had a spiked one, but . . ." He shrugged. ". . . I'm sure we were in a panic as usual, and the important thing was to get the production on. I think that's always been the important thing—to get the production on—and it's never left much time for anything else. Plays are easier, too—I find plays easier than everything else. Other things just get so . . . complicated . . ."

This comment seemed to encompass his whole life. He drooped, exhausted.

"Tony," said Charles very quietly, "why don't you give me the gun?"

There was an instantaneous change as the man's body snapped alert. "Oh no. I may need it."

"What do you mean?"

"There are people out to get me. People who aren't afraid to use violence."

His words sounded like the definitive statement of paranoia.

"But, Tony, you can't go around shooting people."

"Only in self-defense. I hope it won't come to that. I'm sure it won't. But if someone attacks you, you have to defend yourself. Those who offer no resistance get trampled on, and I've been trampled on for long enough."

"Tony—"

"No, Charles. I know what needs to be done. It's all very clear to me now. I know what needs doing, and at last—thank God—I'm ready to do it."

"What do you mean?"

"I mean that all the cheating that's been going on, all the things that have been wrong with this theatre, are about to be sorted out." He sighed, anticipating the relaxation this moment would bring. "Soon it'll all be over. One confrontation . . . if I have the strength to do it . . . and it'll all be over."

This was beginning to sound uncomfortably like a statement of intent to murder. Charles moved forward. "Tony, I think you'd better give me that gun."

"No, I'm sorry. I need it. To protect myself."

Charles stretched out a hand. "Tony. . ."

The noise of the gunshot in the enclosed space was thunderous. Charles heard the lightbulb above him shatter and felt the rain of glass on his shoulders.

He looked for a second at Tony. The man's face seemed to register surprise as he looked at the gun, almost as if the firing had been accidental.

But Charles didn't feel inclined to explore that possibility. The barrel still pointed at him, and he was no hero. He turned and rushed out of the door, slamming it behind him.

He had reached the bottom of the wall-ladder and was at stage level before he realized that there was no sounds of pursuit. He froze for a full minute, then gingerly climbed back up the ladder and on to the cast-iron floor of the gallery. He inched his way towards the prop room door, his ears straining for any unexpected sound.

All he could hear came from down below. "The deaths will not stop at one," Miss Laycock-Manderley was saying. "The forces of evil demand their tool of blood."

He reached the door and, leaning against the adjacent wall in best television detective style, reached for the handle. He gave it a sharp turn and a push.

The door did not shift.

He tried a more forceful shove.

Nothing. The door had been locked from the inside.

He put his ear to it. No sound.

He banged on the door with increasing force. But there was no response.

Then he remembered the other exit from the prop-store, the exit that led to the front of the theatre.

That was the way Tony Wensleigh must have gone, crazed by paranoia, with the gun in his hand.

Straight into the administrative office.

Where he was likely to find the man he saw as his greatest enemy—the Regent Theatre's General Manager—Donald Mason.

ACT THREE

CHAPTER
TWELVE

WHAT MAKES IT all go gruesome," announced James De Meaux, "is the fact that it must all have been planned. Someone worked it all out, every ghastly move."

He stifled a yawn. He really was feeling very tired. Of course, he was playing a major role, and it was the third week, but that shouldn't make him feel so absolutely *drained*. He knew what it was, of course—Nella. Lovely girl, but so inconvenient that she was at *Shove It* rehearsals all day. He could have coped with her very nicely in the afternoons, but all this late night emotion was very wearing. Sex was very nice, he reflected, but not when it interfered with sleep. Be quite a relief, really, to get back to his nice little flat in Pimlico. Have a few days' sleep.

"Yes, but who?" asked Felicity Kershaw. "We're still no nearer to working out who did it."

She was also tired, but happier about it. The guy who'd directed *Scrag End of Neck* at the Bus Depot had turned up to the night before's performance and said she acted like "a real cow," which she had taken as a compliment. He had then let her buy him a meal (including Vanilla Ice Cream) at Mr. Pant's, while he expatiated on the rights of women. He had gone back to her digs, made love to her relentlessly all night and left after breakfast, having borrowed fifty pounds. She felt fulfilled as a woman.

"Well, Colonel Fripp was certainly involved. He must have tampered with the telephone. Why else should be bring that great array of screwdrivers in his luggage?"

"But he didn't hang himself. That was the work of his accomplice."

"The mysterious woman."

"Whoever she may be." Felicity Kershaw let out another of her laughs, confident that she was showing exactly what sort of bourgeois cow would be first against the wall, "come the revolution."

James De Meaux looked thoughtful. An infatuated First Fairy had once told him he was very sexy when he looked thoughtful, so he did it whenever possible.

"We've heard from Professor Weintraub's examination of the body that Colonel Fripp probably died between four and five in the afternoon. It might be worth checking what everyone was doing around that time."

"Well, if you want to start with me, darling, my movements were quite simple. I remember exactly. I went for a walk with Miss Laycock-Manderley."

"In the rain?"

"Yes. It was pouring."

"Precisely. Pouring. What makes one thing rather odd."

"What's that?"

"I refer to the fact—" James De Meaux rounded on his fiancée "—that, when you returned from that walk, your overcoat was dripping wet, while Miss Laycock-Manderley's was not even damp."

"Ah," Felicity Kershaw was meant to look trapped, and expressed this by clutching her stomach.

"Do you have any explanation of that for me, Felicity?"

"Well . . ."

"Or let me put it another way—what evil hold has Miss Laycock-Manderley over you that would make you lie to provide her with an alibi?"

Then followed one of Leslie Blatt's favorite dramatic devices, which was used liberally throughout his work. Just at the point when a character had asked a relevant question, one that threatened to unravel the plot a little, another character would enter and prevent the answer being spoken.

In this case, the interruption came from Lady Hilda De Meaux. She swept on in her Act Three pearl grey silk dress (Tony had put his foot down, but she had overruled him) and recited, "I thought we could all do with a drink, so I've asked Wilhelmina to bring them in here."

As she said this, she decided definitely that Sylv would wear a midnight-blue silk dress for Act Two of *Shove It*. That's what the character would do. She was, after all, going to appear in public, in the court, and Sylv was the sort of person to really care about her appearance under such circumstances. If she wore that thing Wardrobe had provided, she would look less smart than the two policewomen who flanked her in the dock. That wouldn't do. No, midnight-blue definitely. She would speak to Tony.

"What a good idea, Lady Hilda," said Felicity Kershaw, glad of the change of subject. "It's not my usual drink, but I could do with a large whisky after all this."

"I think I might join you in *one*," agreed James De Meaux. He'd tried putting the emphasis on every separate word of that line, and none of them sounded right. Tonight's experiment, hitting the "one," seemed no more successful than the others.

Wilhelmina appeared in the doorway with a silver salver bearing the impedimenta of whisky and sherry decanters, soda syphon and cut-glass tumblers. "Where would you like me to put these, milady?" she asked.

Her mind supplied an obscene suggestion to answer the question. She was now even more tired, the midnight excursions with her factory-owner having continued through the run of the play. She was also disgruntled that he had made no further reference to the West Indies, and wondered whether he had been spinning her a line all the time. On top of that, her period was a couple of days late, which was all she needed.

"Oh, over by the fireplace, thank you, Wilhelmina. And

would you like to call Professor Weintraub and Miss Laycock-Manderley?''

''No need in my case. I am here already,'' said the Professor, leaping friskily through the French windows.

Three more performances, he was thinking. Get this one finished and then there are only three more. Then, first thing on Sunday morning, shake the dust of Rugland Spa off my feet and get back to Jerome and the chihuahuas.

''I wonder,'' mused James De Meaux thoughtfully, because Leslie Blatt had to fill in the hiatus till Miss Laycock-Manderley's entrance with something, ''if there's any way we could make contact with the police. Do you think they'd see, mater, if I did semaphore from the tower?''

''With the weather like this?'' asked Lady Hilda rhetorically. The man in charge of Sound tweaked up his volume control and it rained heavily. ''They'd never see you, James. When the wind's coming up from the sea, the Grange is virtually invisible from Winklesham.''

''Oh, just an idea.''

Wilhelmina returned. ''Miss Laycock-Manderley will not be a moment, milady. She is just powdering her nose.''

If I actually am pregnant, she was thinking, I could tell him it's his (which it quite possibly could be) and maybe he'd marry me. Hmm, on the other hand, he has already got a grown-up family. And he doesn't really give the impression that children are any longer what he wants from a woman. Have to ask him directly tonight about the West Indies, at least find out where I stand.

''Thank you, Wilhelmina. Would you care to serve the drinks?''

''Yes, milady.''

''[AD LIB SERVING DRINKS DURING THE ENSUING DIALOGUE]'' it said in the script, which is always a risky thing (and often a lazy thing) for a playwright to write, because actors vary so much in their improvisational skills. Some are struck dumb, as soon as they have to leave the printed text, while others seize the opportunity to weave elaborate fantasies, build in complicated sub-plots which bear no relation to the main action. Without a strong directorial hand, chaos can ensue.

But Anthony Wensleigh's had never been a strong directorial hand. And Felicity Kershaw saw the stage direction as an opportunity to aggrandize her part and to make more of a political statement. On this particular night, fired by the militancy of the director who had spent the night with her, she embroidered more than usual.

"Oh, a sherry for me. Just a teensy-weensy sherry. I do hope it's South African. I really do so approve of South Africa—at least it's an ordered society. Like it used to be here. Till all these trade unions started to take over with all their unhealthy leftist talk . . ." She thought that was probably sufficient to make her ironic point and cause discomfort amongst any plutocrats in the audience who would realize that they were being pilloried, so she returned to the line they had rehearsed. "Yes, just a small sherry, please."

The trouble with that sort of ad libbing is that the "ensuing dialogue," the dialogue which is meant to be heard, is lost completely. But since this main dialogue conformed to Leslie Blatt's usual standard, it didn't matter that much.

When they were all supplied with drinks, Lady Hilda raised her sherry glass and said, "What is the toast to be?"

This was the cue for the spectral entrance of Miss Laycock-Manderley, with the line, "How about absent friends?"

But Miss Laycock-Manderley did not appear. There was an ugly pause.

"Um, how about 'Cheers'?" offered Felicity Kershaw, trying to save the situation.

"Or 'Prost!'?" suggested Professor Weintraub, rather overdoing the character bit.

" 'Your good health' maybe?" was Lady Hilda's suggestion.

James De Meaux realized it was one of those awful moments when he ought to *do* something. Everyone else had had a go; he had to come up with something. "What about 'Bottoms Up', mater? 'Down the hatch' . . . ? 'Here's mud in your eye' . . . ? Um . . ."

He was saved from further meanderings through *The Book of Your Favorite Toasts* by the belated appearance of Miss Laycock-Manderley. She was meant to look spectral at this point, but it was a shock to all the cast just how spectral she looked. She was in a state of shock, wide-eyed and trembling.

"How about . . ." she quavered, ". . . absent friends?"

"I find that in rather bad taste, Miss Laycock-Manderley," rebuked Lady Hilda, homing in again on Leslie Blatt's text.

"Simply honoring the dead, Lady Hilda." Miss Laycock-Manderley's teeth were chattering now, as she continued, "And those about to die."

Lady Hilda looked at her curiously. "Would you care for a drink, Miss Laycock-Manderley?"

"Yes, please. A small sherry would be most welcome."

Looks more like she needs a massive brandy, thought Wilhelmina, as she poured out the apple juice.

"Or, no—I think I'll have a whisky."

Wilhelmina changed decanters and started to pour the cold tea.

"What did you mean, Miss Laycock-Manderley, when you spoke of 'those about to die'?"

"Ha, Lady Hilda. Do you really believe we have seen the last death of this weekend at Wrothley Grange?" As she spoke, she swayed, threatening to fall.

Wilhelmina took the cold tea across to her. *'Are you all right?'* the maid hissed.

"Terrible news. Just heard backstage," was all that could be hissed back before Lady Hilda had finished saying, "I think you're being overdramatic, Miss Laycock-Manderley."

"I wish you were right, Lady Hilda. Excuse me . . ." She fumbled in her handbag. "I have a slight headache and will just take one of my pills."

"You can't be serious about more deaths." Felicity Kershaw clutched at her vitals as she spoke.

"On yes." Elaborately Miss Laycock-Manderley put a pill in her mouth and tried to wash it down with cold tea. Her hand was shaking so much the liquid slopped all over her dress.

"What on earth's up with her?" James De Meaux whispered to his mother.

"The bottle, I would imagine," Lady Hilda replied through closed teeth, before continuing, "No, I think the sequence of deaths has ended. What is more, I think that James and I know who is responsible for them. Perhaps you would like to tell us, Miss Laycock-Manderley, what you were really doing while you were meant to be taking a walk with Miss Kershaw?"

"What?" Miss Laycock-Manderley's hand flew to her throat. Given the state she was in, it was hard to tell whether this was acting or not.

"And also," James De Meaux chipped in, "what you were actually doing at the time of my father's death in the library?"

"I don't know what you are talking about." She started to sway and totter. She was meant to sway and totter at this point in the play, but the rest of the cast, who had never seen her sway and totter before in quite the same way, watched, mesmerized.

"Are you all right, Miss Laycock-Manderley?"

"No, I . . . er . . ." With another clutch at her throat, she slumped down on to a convenient sofa.

Wilhelmina knelt beside her and loosened her collar. *"For Christ's sake, what happened?"*

"It's awful. I just heard . . ."

"WHAT?" Wilhelmina hissed in frustration, as she felt the slumped finger's pulse.

"Is she all right, Wilhelmina?"

"The maid rose. "She's dead, milady."

"Good God!" James De Meaux crossed over to them. "Are you sure?"

"Certain."

James De Meaux picked up the bottle from which Miss Laycock-Manderley had taken the pill and sniffed it.

Wilhelmina, to the surprise of the rest of the cast, because she had never done it before, again knelt down by the latest victim of the Wrothley Grange murderer. *"Tell me what's happened!"*

"Cyanide," James De meaux announced with the air of a connoisseur of fine wines.

Miss Laycock-Manderley's lips didn't move as she murmured the news. *"Tony Wensleigh's shot himself"*

"Good God," said James De Meaux.

And Leslie Blatt's dialogue showed more sense of dramatic timing than usual as he went on. "It was suicide!"

CHAPTER
__THIRTEEN__

"WHY DID YOU find the body, Mr. Paris?"

"Why?" The detective game him a long-suffering look. "Oh, I'm sorry, I see what you mean. You mean why did I go up to the administrative office in the middle of a performance?"

"Precisely."

"I went because I was worried about what Tony was going to do."

"You suspected that he might be about to kill himself?"

"No. I suspected that he might be about to kill someone else."

The detective sighed. There is no natural affinity between policemen and actors. With an expression of long-suffering, he asked, "Who did you think he was about to kill?"

"Perhaps I'd better explain from the beginning."

"That might help."

Briefly Charles outlined his encounter with the Artistic Director in the props store, concluding. "Because he was waving the gun around and talking about ending the pressure and sorting things out, I thought he meant he was going to commit murder . . . but I see now that most of what he said could have referred to suicide."

"Yes. You hadn't had a quarrel in the props store?"

Charles looked bewildered. "No. What made you ask that?"

The detective became fascinated by the end of his pencil. "Oh, I don't know. I just thought you might have been friends and . . . you know . . . had an argument and he might have . . . ."

Oh, I see. The old all-actors-are-gay syndrome. The detective was trying to find a lovers' tiff as an explanation for the suicide.

"No. If you're looking for a motive, I'm afraid you don't have to be as devious as that. Tony Wensleigh was under a lot of pressure in his job. There was a Boarding Meeting planned for tomorrow evening, when it seemed likely that certain questions were going to be raised about his running of the theatre."

The detective looked interested for the first time. This sounded like something he could understand. "What, you mean he'd got his hand in the till, he was ripping the theatre off?"

Though this coincided closely with Charles' conjecture, he had no proof and reckoned the dead deserved some loyalty. "I don't know."

"But this meeting was going to put him on the spot?"

"Certainly. It was the culmination of a long, unhappy period of conflict."

"Conflict with who?"

"With the theater's General Manager, Donald Mason. They had rather different methods of running the Regent and I think these were going to be discussed at tomorrow's meeting."

"And you reckon this Mason had caught Wensleigh on the fiddle?"

"I don't know. You'd have to ask Donald."

"Yes, I'll do that. But, anyway, this meeting tomorrow looked like a being a showdown?"

"Yes."

"So, if Wensleigh knew he was going to lose, that'd give him the perfect motive for suicide." The detective sounded pleased to have got that sorted out so quickly.

"It might do," said Charles cautiously.

"And when you said you thought he was intending to murder someone, you were thinking of this Donald Mason."

"Yes. But I misunderstood him rather seriously."

"Hmm. Could we just go through your movements again, after your conversation in the props store?"

"Okay. Well, after he fired the gun at me—"

"Do you think he did actually intend to hit you?"

"No, I don't. I did at the time, which was why I ran out, but, in retrospect, I don't think he even intended to fire it. He looked very surprised when the gun went off."

"Right. But you ran, anyway . . . ?"

"Yes. I got right down as far as the stage. Then, since he obviously wasn't following me, I went back up again."

"Why?"

"To talk with him further. To reason with him. He was obviously in a very emotional state. I thought I might be able to help him."

"Hmm."

"But when I got up there, I found the props store door locked, so I assumed that he had gone forward to the administrative office."

"Where he shot himself."

"Yes."

"But you thought he was going forward to commit a murder."

"Yes, I was wrong. It was just that Donald Mason was quite likely to be in the office."

"But he wasn't."

"I gather not. I met him backstage later and he'd been there most of the evening."

"I see. So let's just get the time-scale sorted out. After you'd found the props store locked, what did you do?"

"I went back down the ladder and then, after a bit, I went around the outside of the theatre, in through the front doors and up the stairs to the administrative office."

" 'After a bit', Mr. Paris?"

"Yes, well, I wasn't quite sure what to do next. I went to my dressing room for a moment. I . . . dithered."

"You thought a murder was about to take place and you dithered?"

"Yes."

The detective did not add any verbal comment to this; it seemed unnecessary.

"So how long would you say elapsed between your last seeing Wensleigh in the props store and finding his body?"

"Ten, fifteen minutes. I know when I went out of the Stage Door to go around the front, they were just getting to the end of Act Two, just about to do the hanging. And I remember a line I heard while I was up in the gallery, so we could work it out exactly from the running time of the play."

"Probably won't be necessary, but it might be useful. So let's move on to when you got to the administrative office. Was everything exactly as when we arrived?"

"Yes. It was clear what had happened. There was so much blood, I could see he was dead, so I didn't touch him. I didn't touch anything."

"Not even the telephone?"

"No. I phoned for the police from backstage. I thought I should tell someone official before I contacted you, so I went back backstage and found Donald. In fact, Councilor Inchbald was also there, so I was able to tell him."

"Right. Could you just describe Wensleigh's posture when you found him?"

"He was sitting in his chair, slumped forward over the desk. The top drawer of the desk was slightly open. There was blood everywhere. The gun was in his right hand—or rather half out of his right hand, lying on the desk."

"That sounds about right. And you didn't read the note?"

"I didn't see a note, let alone read it."

"Ah." The detective took out of his file a polythene bag containing a white Regent Theatre envelope. "It was in the drawer."

"I see. What did it say?"

"I'm afraid I don't think I should really tell you that, Mr. Paris. There is a certain privacy about these things. If you were his widow, of course you should see it, but . . ."

"Okay, don't worry." Charles looked at the detective. "It was a suicide note, I take it?"

"I think there's little doubt about that, Mr. Paris. Self-recrimination, apologies for his life . . . Always a great relief when they do leave a note—makes our job easier." The detective rose. "You've been most helpful, thank you. I've got to talk to other people, obviously, and may need to ask you a few supplementary questions."

"Fine."

"And you'll almost definitely be required for the inquest."

"Yes. Any idea when that's likely to be?"

"Next few days. Can't say exactly."

"Okay."

The detective rubbed his hands. "No, this is really a very satisfactory case, as suicides go. Clear statement of intent from the victim—though in fact you misunderstood it. Clear motive, in that he was building up to a crunch meeting which threatened his career. And, just to put the cherry on the cake, a nice note, as well. All in all, nice, straightforward little suicide."

Frank Walby made it to Fleet Street again on the Friday morning. Just.

He had been seized by the hold-the-front-page glamor of the suicide at the Regent Theatre, talked to anyone who would talk to him there, used his contacts in the local police and, with a bottle of whisky by his typewriter just like in the movies, hammered out a dramatic couple of columns for the national press.

He had then run it through to an old Fleet Street contact, now a night editor, and finished the bottle of whisky in celebration of his scoop.

The next morning the story appeared, subbed down to two lines, without Frank Walby's by-line. It was dropped completely from later editions.

No one really expected there to be a rehearsal for *Shove It* on the Friday morning, so most of the cast went down to the theatre to see if there was any notice on the Green Room board to tell them what to do.

There was. Donald Mason was too efficient to allow his company to go wandering around like lost sheep, whatever the disruption. A meeting would be held on stage at eleven o'clock to outline future plans. The company sat around until then making coffee and comparing previous theatrical disasters. Laurie Tichbourne told how he had once played Rosencrantz with a cracked bone in his toe, "undiagnosed for *a whole week.*"

Charles wandered around restlessly backstage. He had slept badly and was still in a state of mind shock after discovering Tony's body. Mimi's so-called kedgeree hadn't helped. He also felt a pang of useless guilt. If only he'd understood what Tony had been saying, he might have been able to do something to prevent the suicide. If only . . . sometimes he reckoned that's what he should have engraved on his tombstone.

He met Donald Mason, who was just finishing a conversation on the backstage pay-phone. The General Manager grimaced as he put the receiver down. "Just ringing around the Board members to tell them the meeting's off. Not an ideal place to work from."

"Police still checking out your office?"

"Yes. Say I may be able to get back in late this afternoon. It's a bloody nuisance, though. All the files I need are up there."

"Yes."

"I should be ringing around to try and find a new director to come in and salvage *Shove It.*"

"Yes, of course. I hadn't thought of that."

"I mean, I don't think we'll manage to open on Wednesday, but if we could just postpone for a couple of days . . . The one thing we mustn't do is have the theater dark. That'd be playing right into the hands of the anti-theater lobby. Have to be seen to be doing something, or the Regent's finished."

"You're right. Did you have a long session with the police?"

"Not that long. They seemed to think everything was pretty cut and dried. It's an absolute disaster, though. It never occurred to me that Tony'd do something like that. And I feel terrible for hounding him so much. I was just trying to make him a bit more efficient, get the theatre back on to an even keel . . . Now I almost feel as if I've driven him to it."

"I feel I should have been able to stop him too."

"Yes." The General Manager sighed. "Poor old Tony. He was inefficient—and possibly even worse—but he really did care about the Regent. As much as I do. I suppose the best I can do for his memory is to ensure that the theatre survives—and make it as successful as it's in my power to make it."

Herbie Inchbald addressed the eleven o'clock meeting. The little man with the mane of hair took his responsibilities as Chairman of the Regent Board seriously, and obviously enjoyed giving his team-talks, even under such clouded circumstances.

"I think you'll all have heard by now what happened last night. I was one of the first to hear the news backstage, and if you're feeling the same sort of shock as I'm still feeling, I know you must be pretty shaken.

"I'm sure I speak for all of us when I say how upset I am about Tony's death. We all appreciated him as a director and friend, and I only wish that we had recognized the symptoms of the breakdown which was coming and which led him to . . . do what he did. But Tony was a reticent chap, didn't talk a lot about his feelings.

"But we can't look to the past. The time will come for a memorial service for Tony, when we can all voice our appreciation of him, but at the moment our first priority is to get on with the work of the theatre.

"You probably know by now—and I'm not pretending otherwise—that the Regent has been going through a fairly rough time recently, and this new disaster couldn't have come at a worse moment. The town's full of people who don't give a damn about the Arts, and, if we have to close the theatre down, they'll do their level best to see that it doesn't reopen.

"So we must keep going. *Shove It* will open, don't

worry. May take us a day or two to find a new director, but it will open—you take my word.

"So I must ask you all to be patient and co-operative, and we'll let you know as soon as there's anything *to* let you know. Meanwhile, there's a performance tonight and two more tomorrow of *The Message Is Murder*. And the best tribute you can all give to the memory of Tony Wensleigh is to make sure that all three performances of his last production are real little crackers!"

The Councilor's experience again told, and he secured his required round of applause.

There was no question about the commitment of the General Manager and the Chairman of the Board. Charles wondered whether, after all, Tony's death might not prove a blessing to the Regent Theatre. His financial irregularities would probably now never be investigated, and his departure had cleared the air. The new Artistic Director, when he was appointed, would start with a clean slate and, given the back-up of Donald's efficiency and, presumably, better judgment than Tony had demonstrated, might well be able to lead the theatre into a new era of success.

Assuming, of course, that the Regent could survive the hazardous period of interregnum.

He had given his all (insofar as a dead body is capable of giving its all) in the Friday night performance and was unscrewing the sword from his chest, when there was a tap on the dressing room door and Nella entered.

"Charles, there's a lady at the Stage Door who would like to speak to you."

"Oh?"

"She looks upset. Could you come down?"

"Do you know who it is?"

"I'm not sure, but I think it's Tony's widow."

She did look upset, but seemed to be in control. She introduced herself as Martha Wensleigh, and agreed to his suggestion that they should go over to the pub and have a drink. Even on Friday night, he assured her, it would be pretty empty at this time.

As they crossed the bar, the old lady with the Guinness, who seemed as much a fixture as the dart-board, claimed to recognize them both, but Charles ushered the new widow past to a sheltered corner. He had a large Bell's and she agreed to his suggestion of a large brandy.

"I'm very sorry," he began conventionally.

"Thank you. I haven't really started to feel yet."

"No. It'll take time. He was a fine man." The clichés jolted out uneasily. He wondered how much Martha knew of what had brought her husband to his death. It struck him that in the three weeks he had been in Rugland Spa, he had never heard Tony's wife even mentioned. She hadn't been at the first night party, and the fact that Nella had been uncertain in identifying her suggested that she was not often at the theatre. This was unusual; in most of the provincial theatres he had worked where the Artistic Director had a wife, Charles had been aware of her presence. (In one particular company he couldn't avoid it, because she played all the female leads.) Maybe the Wensleigh's marriage was breaking up.

Martha scotched the idea straight away, by saying, "Tony and I were very close."

"Ah."

"He wasn't very outgoing to people he didn't know, but he talked to me. Whenever he got the time, he talked."

"Yes." The conversation wasn't really flowing. "He can't have had much time. The Regent was a very demanding job."

She nodded. "Sometimes it seemed he only came home to sleep. Sometimes not even that. All-night lighting, that sort of thing."

"Of course." Charles wondered if she had disliked the theatre, kept away from it deliberately as some mark of disapproval.

Again she answered his unspoken question. "Tony liked to keep his work and his home life separate. He gave a lot of himself during the days; and then at home I like to think he could relax, recharge his batteries."

"Yes."

"When we first started living together, I thought he wanted me as part of his work. I used to do Wardrobe. But then it was clear he valued me more as someone outside it all, someone who could be objective, who wasn't involved in all the ups and downs of productions and politics."

Charles nodded. He knew a lot of people in the business who kept their marriages and sanity intact that way. Choosing a partner outside the theatre and you've got someone with whom you can laugh about the obsessive dramas and crises of rehearsal and performance. If you ever see them . . . That had been the problem with Frances all those years before. He was never there, always off in the alien single beds of the nation's Mimis. Acting and marriage had different imperatives, which were hard to reconcile.

Martha Wensleigh broke into his maudlin reverie with an abrupt change of subject. "I thought of you because of something I heard from a man called Spike."

"Spike?"

"His real name was Gareth Warden. He stage-managed at the Regent a few years back."

"Oh, I remember him." It came back. Spike had worked on the pre-London tour of the musical *Lumpkin!*, a show whose progress had been bedeviled by a series of unexplained crimes.

"Spike talked about you one night when he was a bit drunk. Said you were not above a bit of detective investigation."

"What a nice way of putting it."

"I want you to undertake an investigation for me."

"Into Tony's death?"

"Yes."

Charles looked at the widow with pity. "I think I'm unlikely to unearth a satisfying murderer. There seems to be little doubt that he did kill himself."

"I know that. I don't want you to unearth a murderer. I just want to know what drove him to . . . do what he did."

Strange, that she should use exactly the same euphemism

as Herbie Inchbald. Or perhaps not strange. Anything rather than define the unpalatable truth too closely.

"Tony had been under a lot of pressure for a long time," said Charles gently. "I think he was very confused."

"You don't have to tell me that, Charles. I lived with him."

"Yes. Of course. What I'm saying is, I think that confusion impaired his judgment. He had done a series of strange things recently. I'm afraid taking his own life may have been the culmination of these. What's the phrase—'while the balance of his mind was disturbed'?"

"Yes, but what disturbed it?"

Charles shrugged. "As I say, a series of things, The Regent's been under threat for a long time, you know that—that was one continuing pressure. Then . . ." Charles fought shy of mentioning the financial fiddles and the attempted murders. "There were other things," he ended lamely.

"But he used to be able to cope with pressure."

"One day it just gets too much, He had been getting worse—forgetting he had done things, not doing things he thought he'd done . . ."

"He talked about that. It worried him a lot. There were letters he swore he had written, and then it turned out he hadn't . . . very strange . . ."

"He was always at rehearsal," Charles explained soothingly. "Administration was never one of his strengths."

"I know that. But what I do want to find out is what the final pressure was. What made him . . . do it."

"Didn't he talk to you about it?"

"Only in general terms. He said he didn't want to go into details until he'd sorted everything out. And I thought he had. He rang me the evening he died."

"Did he?" Charles was instantly alert. "Have you told the police?"

"Oh yes," she replied wearily.

"What time did he ring?"

"About eight."

Before Charles had met him in the prop store. "And what did he say?"

"He said he'd finally sorted it out. He said it had all been very confusing, but he was getting there. Soon he'd have it all taped and the pressure would be off."

Charles grimaced ruefully. "That's pretty much what he said to me later on. It's ambiguous, to say the least."

"Yes. The police . . ."

"I can imagine. Took it as further evidence that he intended to do away with himself."

"Yes." Martha Wensleigh looked discouraged and, for the first time, as if she was about to break down.

"He didn't say anything else, anything more specific?"

"He said something rather strange. I can't remember the exact words, but, more or less, he said, 'At least I'm not paranoid. A paranoid *thinks* he's being persecuted, but now I *know* I've been being persecuted.' "

"I'm afraid that's exactly what a paranoid would say."

He hadn't said it gently enough. Martha Wensleigh flared up. "Oh, for God's sake! Can't you say anything more helpful than that?"

"I'm sorry."

She looked at him. Her eyes had the same dark vulnerability as her husband's. Grey-haired lady in her fifties, not particularly attractive. And now a widow. What did the rest of her life hold for her?

She swallowed down a sob as she spoke carefully. "I'm sorry too. It's just that Tony was convinced someone was out to get him, and someone at the Regent was trying to ruin his career. He said it more than once. He didn't say who, and he didn't say how—just that someone was out to destroy him and the theatre."

"I'm sorry to have to say it, Martha, but that again sounds very like paranoia."

"Yes, I agree. I could. But I sort of got the impression that Tony was building up some sort of case against his . . . enemy. When he rang last night, I thought he meant his case was complete."

Charles looked sufficiently dubious for her to lose her temper again. "Oh, you're just like everyone else! You don't want to help and—"

"I do. It's just . . ."

"Forgive me." Once again she made a supreme effort to control herself. "As I said, I'm not feeling properly yet. Not feeling the things I will feel. Soon I'm going to break down and weep for a year. But at the moment all that's coming out is anger, anger and the need to do something, I can't bring Tony back, but at least I can find out who persecuted him so much that he killed himself. Or if I can't . . ." She softened, and for the first time Charles was aware of her as a woman, as someone with a sexual identity, "perhaps you can."

The appeal was strong, and he would have liked to agree to what she asked. But he felt certain that she was going to be disappointed in her quest, and thought it better that that disappointment come sooner rather than later.

"Martha, from what I can gather, Tony had been cracking up for some long time. His artistic judgment seemed to have gone."

"What do you mean?"

"Well, I don't know when the season's program is decided . . ."

"Oh, about eight months back. Has to be finalized around June."

"Then I reckon he had started to crack back in June. Do you really think that choosing *The Message Is Murder*, followed by *Shove It*, is the action of someone whose artistic judgment is intact?"

Martha Wensleigh stared at him, surprised so dominating her face that it drove out the pain and distress. "But he didn't want to do those plays."

"What?"

"Tony thought they were both awful. Directing them made him utterly miserable."

"Then why on earth did he choose them?"

"He didn't. That's done by the Play Selection Committee."

"Isn't he even on the committee?"

"Oh yes, but he could be overruled by the others."

"Who are the others?"

"The Chairman of the Theatre Board, the General Manager, and there's always a Creative Consultant. This year it was Leslie Blatt."

CHAPTER
FOURTEEN

CHARLES HAD to parry offers of tea, coffee, cocoa and rock cakes from Mimi before he could get to bed and look at the file that Martha Wensleigh had given him.

It was her revelation about Tony's dislike of the plays that had persuaded him to go further. So much of his thinking about the collapse of the Artistic Director's judgment had been based on the two choices that he now felt the whole case needed re-examination. Also, the knowledge that Wensleigh's opinion of *The Message Is Murder* and *Shove It* coincided with his own made him feel closer to the dead man than he ever had during their acquaintance.

So he had agreed that he would investigate, but with no very lively hope of success. It was the nakedness in Martha Wensleigh's eyes that had swayed him, though deep down he suspected he would find out nothing that was not already obvious.

The file she had brought with her was all that Tony had kept at home. Any hope that it would prove to be some kind of dossier, evidence in the "case" his wife had suspected he was building up against his "enemy," was soon dashed.

The file was a further demonstration of Tony Wensleigh's disorganized mind, of his lack of administrative ability. It

was just bits and pieces, carbons of letters and photocopies
of documents jumbled up with photos of actors, program
proofs, rehearsal notes scribbled in his cramped handwrit-
ing, props lists, snippings of Frank Walby reviews, Board
Meeting agendas, designers' sketches for sets, phone num-
bers on backs of envelopes, restaurant bills and other less
decipherable scraps.

There was no system in the collection; it was as if the
Artistic Director had every now and then emptied out his
jacket pockets and shoved whatever he found into the file.

Just sorting through the mass of paper would be a long
job. Charles was glad he had taken the precaution of buying
a half-bottle of Bell's from the pub. He took a long swig
and, propping himself up on Mimi's brushed nylon pillows,
started to wade through.

After about an hour, he had winnowed out four single
sheets and one stapled bunch of papers which he thought
might have some bearing on the case, or which, failing that,
might at least provide some background to recent events at
the Regent Theatre.

The first confirmed what his widow had said about Tony
Wensleigh's view of the plays in the current season. It was a
duplicated sheet, headed "Play Selection Committee—
Proposals," containing a list of play titles. Presumably,
since there were only seventeen in all, these represented
some sort of short list. Five shows in the season, no
argument about the pantomime (which had been *Puss In
Boots* that year) and it, seemed, one nomination from each
committee member for each of the other four slots.

It was clear, from his underlinings and comments, which
had been the Artistic Director's own suggestions. *Much Ado
About Nothing, Sleuth, Kiss Me Kate* and Ayckbourn's *Ten
Times Table*. Not wildly original, perhaps, but a fairly
well-balanced program of Rugland Spa fodder.

What was striking about the committee's voting was that
in every case the Artistic Director's proposals had been
voted out, and in each case replaced with something inferi-
or. Even *Much Ado . . .* had given way to *All's Well That*

Ends Well, a much more difficult and less readily accessible play.

Whether the committee's voting reflected lack of artistic judgment or something more sinister it was hard to be certain. The first was quite possible, Charles reflected. He already had serious doubts about Herbie Inchbald's knowledge of the theater; *The Message Is Murder* did not inspire much confidence in Leslie Blatt as an arbiter of taste; and, he suddenly realized, though he had heard Donald Mason talking about a lot of administrative matters, he had never heard an artistic judgment from the General Manager.

On the other hand, the unanimity of voting against Tony Wensleigh suggested that his suspicion of organized opposition was not completely fanciful.

The Artistic Director's view of one of the plays ultimately selected was left in no doubt by a carbon of a letter dated a few days before the Play Selection Committee Meeting.

Dear Leslie [it ran], thank you very much indeed for letting me see the script of *The Message Is Murder*, which I return herewith.

I am afraid your submitting it puts me in a difficult position, because, having known you so long, I would like to be able to write back with enthusiasm, but I'm afraid I can't. I am sure that, as you say, the play was well received when first produced in the fifties, though I feel the fact that its run ended on its pre-London tour may suggest that it lacked a certain West End gloss.

Anyway, that need not matter. Frequently a revival can completely change a play's fortunes. But I'm afraid I cannot see that happening in this case. To be brutally frank, the play has dated badly and now seems painfully contrived. The characters have no inner life or psychological continuity, and, speaking as a director, I can foresee massive problems in giving the play any credibility at all.

I am sorry to have to write this, but I feel that it is better to be frank at this point than by politeness to get caught in a project which should not have started.

Please rest assured that I have often had occasion to
respect your judgment in the past, and am sure that I will
be grateful for your advice in the future. I am only sorry
that I cannot agree with you about the suitability of *The
Message Is Murder* for production at the Regent in the
1980s.

Yours sincerely,
Tony.

The letter interested Charles a lot, not only because it
confirmed Tony Wensleigh's dislike of the play, but also
because it revealed a core of good sense and professional
skill which he had not seen during his brief acquaintance
with the director. Tony Wensleigh might have cracked up in
the intervening months, but he hadn't cracked when he
wrote that letter.

The next document of interest was a letter from Herbie
Inchbald dated some three years previously. It spelled out
precisely the threat to the site of the Regent Theatre.

Dear Tony,

As you know there has been a great deal of toing and
froing on the Council recently over the future of the
Regent and, both as a Councilor and as Chairman of the
Theatre Board, I think it's up to me to keep you informed
of developments.

As you don't need telling, the theatre holds a prime
position in the Maugham Cross area, the whole of which
is badly run down and will at some point require redevelopment. I don't question that that will have to happen in
time, but what I and my supporters on the Council are
trying to ensure is that any development plans guarantee
the survival of the Regent in its current form. As you
have probably gathered, not everyone on the Council
agrees with me. Like everything else, it has become a
political matter, and we're spending an awful lot of
Council time debating the merits of theatre v. Leisure
Center and God knows what else.

The issue has become more pressing, because we have

now had a definite offer on the whole Maugham Cross area from Schlenter Estates. It is an attractive offer and the majority of the Council favor accepting it and appointing Schlenter Estates as developer. They seem to be well backed and have presented us with convincing plans, demonstrating how they will raise development money from a pension fund, etc. They seem to know what they're on about.

And Rugland Spa could use the money. Apart from a guaranteed minimum income from the project, we would also receive a healthy percentage of the gross rents for the completed development, just the sort of financial boost we need in these straitened times. And, of course, we would control the way the development is done, to keep it in tone with the rest of the town center.

But Schlenter do want the Regent site as part of their development, and I think they'd be prepared to do anything to get it. I've already had the soft soap treatment from them, invitations to look around one of their completed projects near Birmingham. I went along, out of curiosity. Most of the day was spent being whisked between expensive restaurants in Rolls-Royces, being fed to the gills with excellent food and champagne (and with a fairly unambiguous offer of a girl at the end of the day if I fancied it). Well, of course, they'd backed the wrong horse with me. I can recognize a bribe a mile off, and am fortunately sufficiently comfortable not even to be tempted. But it does show how important the development is to them, and what they'd be prepared to do to get that site.

As I say, a lot of the Council would let them have it without a backward thought, so we're going to have to fight hard to save it.

I'm sure we'll succeed. As we discussed, I've written to Lord Kitestone asking him to be our patron. His name on our notepaper will give us a lot of respectability. And then we must organize public opinion. I'm sure we can guarantee a good outcry when the proposal to demolish the theatre becomes public, and I'm sure we'll be able to stop it. Either the development will go ahead, leaving the

Regent untouched, or else the whole project will be
shelved.

But, even if the second happens, this has been a grim
warning and its the kind of thing that's bound to come up
again. It's down to us to ensure that we maintain such a
high standard of theatre at the Regent that no one even
dares to suggest closing us.

Anyway, I thought you ought to know the state of play.
Rest assured of the continuing support of myself and
anyone else on the Council who I can speak for (and pray
that there won't be a disaster at the elections!)

                    Yours sincerely,
                    Herbie.

The letter confirmed—if it needed confirming—Councilor
Inchbald's whole-hearted backing for the Regent, but it also
defined the reality of the threat to the theatre's future. And
its total reliance on Council support.

That had been three years before. The Regent was still
standing, and the area in which it stood, Charles had
noticed, was, by Rugland Spa's genteel standards, pretty
shabby. So presumably the deal with Schlenter Estates had
not gone through. But the more run-down the Maugham
Cross area became, and the lower the artistic standards of
the Regent fell, the greater became the likelihood of another
similar offer. An offer which, after recent disasters, the
pro-theatre lobby might find difficult to fight off.

Charles then turned his attention to the stapled sheaf of
papers, which turned out to be photocopies of Donald
Mason's c.v. and references when he applied for the post of
General Manager at the Regent Theatre just over a year
before.

These made fascinating reading. Charles realized that he
knew almost nothing about Donald's past. Whereas much of
actors' conversations is spend in asking each other where
they've worked and who with, such questions are rarely
addressed to General Managers. Indeed, in many theatres,
the cast are hardly aware of the General Manager's presence.

Donald Mason has started out in 1970, it appeared, as an estate agent, which, he wrote, "taught me the basic skills of administration without in any way simulating my mind, which was becoming increasingly set on the idea of working in the theatre." Difficulty in finding an opening in this country had led him to try his luck in Australia, where, starting humbly as an Assistant Front of House Manager, he had risen through various companies, until he reached the status of General Administrator at the Kelly Theater in Sydney. Wishing to try his luck again in his native country, he had returned to England six months previously and found, like many before him, that experience abroad did not count for as much as it should. But, determined to build up his career again, he had been prepared to go a few rungs back down the ladder, and accepted a job as Assistant Front of House Manager at the Pavilion Theatre, Darlington. It was from there that he was applying for the Rugland Spa job.

That career history was adequate for the job; what made it exceptional was the quality of the references that accompanied the application. Charles knew that in the theatre a good reference was sometimes a way of getting rid of a member of the administrative staff who didn't fit in, but that could not explain such unanimity of praise as Donald Mason had received from his Australian employers. Charles didn't know the antipodean theatrical scene, so the names didn't mean anything to him, but there was no doubting the enthusiasm of Ralph Johnson of the Theatre Royal, Adelaide, Rich Coleman of the Dominion, Perth, Greg Avon of the Hippodrome, Melbourne, and Jim Vailis of the Kelly Theatre in Sydney. They all praised Donald Mason's administrative skill, tact and general flair for the theatre; and they all very much regretted losing him. The letters made impressive reading. Rugland Spa had been lucky to catch Mason at a low point in his career, because he was clearly destined for higher things.

The final piece of paper from Antony Wensleigh's file was further confirmation not only of Donald's suitability for his job, but also for the Artistic Director's endorsement of the appointment. The duplicated sheet was headed "General Manager Applicants" and dated nearly a year before. There was a list of five names with times half an hour apart, presumably for their final interviews. There were comments beside all the names in Tony's tiny writing, but against Donald Mason's were four asterisks, an exclamation mark and the remark, "This one by a mile!"

So, though conflict seemed to have developed between the Artistic Director and the General Manager, there was no question of Tony having had Donald foisted on him. He had supported the new appointment unreservedly.

If his feelings of persecution were more than fantasy, then the contents of the Artistic Director's file gave no clue as to the identity of his persecutor. There was only the business of play selection, which could perhaps show organized opposition to Tony, and that seemed more likely to be just the workings of innocent philistinism.

A natural instinct for tidiness made Charles drain the half-bottle of Bell's. Then he switched out the light and tried to snuggle into the brushed nylon sheets (though snuggling and brushed nylon sheets don't really go together). The stuff in the file had been interesting, he reflected, but it hadn't really got him any further in what probably wasn't even a case.

"There was a phone message for you this morning," Mimi announced, as Charles tried not to meet his kipper in the eye. What a hell, he thought, for a fish. Being caught is bad enough. Being kippered adds to the agony. But then to have to suffer the final indignity of being cooked by Mimi . . . it made hanging, drawing, and quartering seem humane.

"Who from?"

Disbelief flooded Mimi's face, before drenching her words. "She said she was your wife."

"Why on earth didn't you wake me?"

"Oh, didn't want to disturb you. I said you were sleeping it off."

So that was going to be the regular line, whoever rang while he was asleep. Thank you very much, Mimi. Just wait and see what I write in your Visitors' Book. I will. I really will.

"Am I to ring her back?"

"No. She said she'd leave a message." Mimi stopped, as if that were all she had to communicate, and started further adulterating her tea with tepid water.

"What was the message?"

"Oh. You want to know?"

"Yes."

"Well, you can never be sure. Some of my gentlemen don't want to hear from their wives, tell Mimi not even to admit they're here if their wives ring." She looked at Charles balefully. "You behind on the maintenance?"

"No, I am not. We are not divorced."

"Oh. Happily together, eh?"

Charles restrained himself. "What was the message?"

"She said she couldn't make lunch tomorrow."

The slap of pain made him realize how much he had been looking forward to seeing Frances. Whatever the situation was, however awkward the meeting, he wanted to see her.

"Oh, well . . ." he said miserably.

"But . . ." Mimi took her time, "she said could you make it dinner instead? An early dinner. She's booked for seven-thirty Sunday. If you can't, ring her between six and seven tonight."

Charles felt such a flood of boyish joy at his hope restored that he forgot Mimi's awfulness. "Terrific," he said, rising from the table.

"Now you're not going to leave that lovely kipper, are you?" demanded Mimi.

Charles felt guilty about Martha Wensleigh, guilty about the anguished appeal he had seen in her eyes. He felt he should have something for her, but knew he had nothing to give.

Still, one new idea had come with the morning. It was tiny and undeveloped, but pursuing it would at least give him the illusion of doing something on the widow's behalf.

The thought he had arose from something in Herbie Inchbald's letter about the proposals to redevelop the Maugham

Cross area. The Councilor had made it clear that Schlenter Estates wanted the site very much, and had even tried tentatively to bribe him as a way of getting it. Was it just possible that they had also found a way of putting pressure on Tony Wensleigh, hoping through him to weaken the theatre's status in the town and make their course easier?

It was fanciful, but no more fanciful than a great many of the blind alleys Charles had run up in the course of his detective career.

The trouble was, he knew nothing about the workings of property companies. However, he did have a friend who might be able to help him.

He phoned from a public call-box, wary of Mimi's telescopic ears.

Kate Venables answered. "Charles, what a pleasure to hear from you. Not to say a surprise. Look, I must dash—taking one of the kids out for her riding lesson. I think Gerald's still here—he's just on his way out to play golf. Just a sec. Lovely to hear you." The receiver was put down and Charles heard receding cries of "Gerald!"

Charles could visualize the house in West Dulwich, a beautifully appointed example of 1970s Georgian. Money had been lavished on it like plant food on a Chelsea Flower Show exhibit. Everything was of the best and of the most expensive. Riding lessons for the children, golf for Gerald, facials for Kate—everything perfect, everything money could buy. Occasionally, in reflective moods, Charles tried to imagine just how much money Gerald Venables made, but usually gave up early on in disbelief. There was the basic profit from the highly successful firm of show business solicitors, but that was now only part of a huge investment income. Gerald was one of the few consistently successful "angels" who actually made a profit from putting money into shows; but he also had stakes in television companies, commercial radio stations and God knew what other lucrative projects.

The two had met at Oxford and, in spite of the fact that Charles' annual income probably represented a month's pocket money for Gerald, had remained friends. Part of the reason for this was Gerald's fascination with detection and childlike eagerness to get involved in any investigation that Charles initiated.

That this eagerness remained undiminished was confirmed by his first words when he reached the phone. "Charles, are you on a case?"

"Not sure. I might be."

"You must be. I don't hear from you from one year's end to the next, and when I do, it's always a case. Spill the beans."

"I'm at Rugland Spa."

"Ah, taking an early retirement?"

"No. Thing is, the Artistic Director of the local theatre has just committed suicide."

"But Charles Paris is convinced it was really murder?"

"No, I'm sorry. Nothing so dramatic. Seems no doubt he actually did away with himself. I just want to know why."

"Ah. And you think I can tell you? You overestimate my powers, I'm afraid. I'm not psychic."

"I just want you to find out some information for me."

"Showbiz?"

"No. It's a bit outside your normal field, but I thought you might be able to root something out. It's about a property company."

Gerald didn't immediately reject the idea that he might know something. As Charles had suspected, the solicitor's investments were well diversified.

"Which property company?"

"Schlenter Estates."

Gerald made a little whistle through his teeth. "The original wide-boys."

"You mean they're crooks?"

The solicitor tutted. "You really must learn to moderate your language, Charles. There are laws of slander in this country. Anyway, a crook is someone who has been found guilty of a crime. Schlenter Estates have never been found guilty of anything."

"But . . . ?"

"But nothing. They are now a highly respected company

with international interests. They're even more respectable since they were taken over by Fowler Rose Stillman.''

"They're big, aren't they? Even I've heard of them.''

"Oh yes. Fowler Rose Stillman are very big. And highly respectable.''

"Then why did you refer to Schlenter as wide-boys?''

"I was being indiscreet.''

"Go on, Gerald, don't be coy.''

"Well, it's going back a few years. During the property boom. Around 1970. Then there were a few uncharitable rumors going around about Schlenter. No property companies had a very good reputation around then.''

"Anything specific?''

"On Schlenter? Can't say off the top of my head. I could check around in the office on Monday, ask a few people, if you like.''

"I'd be very grateful.''

"What do you want exactly?''

"Don't know, really.''

"That's helpful.''

"Well, sort of anything about them. Who really owns them, what they do . . . any dirt, certainly.''

"Just that. Uhuh,'' said Gerald with heavy irony. "I'll see what I can do. Where can I contact you?''

Charles had to give Mimi's number. It wasn't private, but at least it wasn't actually in the Regent.

"I'll have to ring either before eleven or else considerably later,'' said Gerald. "I've just remembered I've got a client coming in at eleven. He's joining the National as an Assistant Director and we're going through his contract. That'll mop up lunch—mop up most of the day, actually.''

"I'll stay in till eleven.''

"Fine. Actually you might know him.''

"Your client?''

"Yes. It's Bill Walsingham—have you worked with him?''

"You bet. Bloody marvelous director.''

"Yes.''

"Oh, well, give him my love.''

"Will do.''

"And now I won't keep you from your golf any longer. Hope to hear from you on Monday."

"Do my best. Oh, incidentally, Charles, isn't it good news about Frances?"

The change of subject was too sudden for Charles. "What about her?"

"Well, I mean this new bloke."

"Ah."

"David. Seems an awfully good thing."

"You've met him?"

"Yes. Absolute charmer." Charles didn't say anything. "No, I'm so pleased for both of you really. I mean, it's been obvious for years that you and Frances weren't going to work out. Kate and I had hoped it would when you first split up, but . . . And Frances has needed someone. So now you must feel a lot freer."

"Freer?" Charles echoed.

"Yes, for all those little actresses, eh? No doubt you've got another little cracker on the scene at the moment."

"No doubt," Charles agreed, feeling emptier than he could ever remember.

CHAPTER
FIFTEEN

THE MESSAGE IS MURDER was given its two final performances on the Saturday, and then returned to its vault, surely never to rise again.

Both the matinée and the evening show were subdued, which was hardly surprising, considering the circumstances. The Methuselahs of Rugland Spa clapped politely at the matinée, and a fuller, fractionally younger audience gave exactly the same reaction to the evening show. Charles unbuckled the Waspee belt of his dueling sword for the last time, and vowed to do something unprecedented. He would turn down work. He would tell his agent on the Monday—if anyone else comes offering a part as a dead body, Charles Paris is unavailable.

The end of the show left everyone in limbo. A director had still not been appointed to rescue *Shove It*, so that production's future remained uncertain, and some members of the company were not sure whether they should be doing a full goodbye routine or if they'd all meet up again for rehearsals the following week.

A subdued little party went for a subdued little celebration at The Happy Friend Chinese Restaurant and Takeaway. Mr. Pang welcomed them with his usual impassive smile.

There was little conviviality around the table. Laurie Tichbourne sat beside Nella, looking at her soulfully. A stranger might have seen this as evidence of a love too deep for words, but Charles recognized the plight of someone who just couldn't think of anything to say.

Cherry Robson was there with her factory-owner, though they were in the middle of some complicated row or negotiation. Half-way through the meal, he stormed out and, after two minutes of truculent deliberation, Cherry followed. She wasn't going to let all that money get away so easily.

Leslie Blatt, no doubt to the relief of the females present, was not there.

Rick Harmer and Gay Milner sat either side of Charles, apparently talking to him, but in fact engaged in long individual monologues. Rick was going on about how successful he was going to be, how almost certain he was to get this major television role, apart from getting this television sit com series to write, and how he wasn't really sure whether his agent had big enough ideas for him. What did Charles think?

Gay Milner was talking about sexual relationships and their relevance to their political context. Most of what she said was direct quotation from the director of *Scrag End of Neck* at the Bus Depot, who appeared to have found a new rationale for that oldest of masculine pursuits—how to get sex without responsibility. It was very important that sexual relationships remained egalitarian, Gay quoted. There was, after all, capitalism in sex as well as other forms of property-owning. It was important that relationships should not be limited by the use of glib emotive buzz-words like "love." What did Charles think?

Since he had no thoughts at all on what either of them was talking about, he said nothing, but that did not deter them from continuing to circle round their subjects right through the meal.

At the end Mr. Pang was once again asked what Ice Creams (Various) he had, and once again he said Vanilla.

The Sunday was a twitchy day for Charles. He would have liked to wake very late, but Mimi decided to hoover the landing outside his bedroom at eight o'clock. She seemed to have some in-built monitor which made her hyper-sensitive to her gentlemen's desires; she must have done, otherwise she couldn't so consistently have ensured that they were frustrated.

When she finished hoovering, Charles turned over, still with a good chance of going back to sleep. He achieved this, but after five minutes was woken by a knock on the door and ordered down for what Mimi had the nerve to call an omelette.

He got out as soon as possible and was faced with the prospect of a day to kill in Rugland Spa, a day when the pubs didn't open till twelve or the cinemas till three. At least, thanks to *Shove It* rehearsals, he hadn't seen either of the films that had started on the Thursday. But did he really want to go to *Bambi*? Or *She Lost Her Swedish Knickers*, come to that? (He wondered idly whether Mrs. Feller spend her spare time picketing the cinema or whether she'd given it up as a bad job.)

The day stretched ahead, one of those awful sagging Sundays in rep. In the old days, he remembered, they had been rare. Sundays had meant tech runs and Dress Rehearsals for a Monday opening. But Equity had tightened up the regulations, now there were overtime rates for Sunday working and as a result few theatres did it. Shows opened now on Wednesday, and usually ran two-and-a-half weeks. The old manic days of weekly rep were gone.

He trudged around the streets of Rugland Spa. Anything of interest the town had to offer (and there wasn't much) he had already seen. He felt mournful and self-pitying.

And he knew that part of the reason was the evening that lay ahead. His mind vacillated between desperately wanting to see her and blind panic. At times he contemplated not turning up at all at the hotel. It might be simpler that way.

* * *

The day passed somehow (*Bambi* was actually much better than he'd remembered it), but he still found himself at the Rugland Spa Hotel half an hour too early. But by then his feet were so tired, he couldn't face another aimless circuit of the town. Anyway, at seven o'clock he would be able to get a drink and he felt he was going to need a couple of stiff Bell's to set him up for the evening.

The Rugland Spa Hotel had been built in the days when the spa meant something, when people actually ventured out to Herefordshire to take the waters, when the town was, if not a wildly fashionable resort, at least an active one.

But health fads change and the people who in the nineteenth century might have taken courses of baths were, in the 1980s, jogging, cramming themselves with vegetable fibre or listening in the privacy of their own homes to their biorhythms. And anyone so cranky as actually to want to take the waters would have been frustrated. The baths complex had fallen into disrepair, been declared unsafe in the 1950s, and ten years later been demolished and supplanted by a supermarket.

But the hotel had remained. The site, on the way out of the town towards Ludlow, had been chosen for its proximity to the baths, but a supermarket didn't attract guests in the same way. The hotel was no longer independently run, but had been taken over by one of the smaller chains, who were having a hard job to keep it going. It was built on too grand a scale. A few elderly people liked to stay there, occasional families were lured out from the cities by offers of "Bargain Breaks," some resolute foreigners "doing Britain" might end up there, but there was no continuity of trade. Businessmen and travelers in the area seemed to prefer the anonymous uniformity of the new motel the other side of town, with its color television, in-house video and "conference facilities."

The hotel's exterior reflected its declining popularity. Its former splendor carried an almost shamefaced air. The name, stuck boldly on the fascia in large metal letters, had tarnished and the "L" dangled diagonally. Creeper threatened to swallow up whole wings and the paintwork on the finely shaped windows was cracked and stained.

It was, thought Charles, as he entered the apologetic portico, another site suitable for development.

He had checked in the car-park for Frances' yellow Renault, but there was no sign of it, so he went straight through to what was called "The Kitestone Bar."

At seven o'clock on a Sunday it was almost uninhabited. And trade they did get on Sundays tended to be lunchtimes; there were still local farmers and wealthy sons of retired parents who believed in bringing family parties out for "Roast beef, Yorkshire pudding, the full works." But the evening trade was very slack.

There was only one other customer, sitting in a bay window, so Charles had no difficulty in engaging the attention of the adolescent barman. That young man, looking, in a red braided jacket too big for him, like a pen in an envelope, had a bit of difficulty in locating the Bell's whisky, but compensated for this by pouring out a huge measure and charging for a single.

The evening was pleasant, so Charles wandered over to the window. As he sat down, he realized that he recognized the bar's other customer.

"Excuse me," he said, moving across to her, "but it's Mrs. Inchbald, isn't it?"

The pudgy face looked up at him. "Oh . . . er . . . We met at the theatre, didn't we?"

"Charles Paris."

"Of course."

"Do you mind if I join you? I'm waiting for my wife," he added quickly, lest she should think his intentions anything but honorable. No doubt even so far a lady as Velma Inchbald regarded herself as a potential target for a predatory male.

"Oh, do, please." The slight exaggeration in her speech and the wide gesture which accompanied it suggested that the pink gin in front of her was not the first she had had that day.

"Herbie," she explained, "is up in London."

"Ah."

"A weekend conference, related to his business," she said importantly.

"Road haulage?"

She looked a little put out to have her husband's business so precisely defined, but conceded that this was so. And she quickly regained any social ground that might have been lost by saying, "Of course, it's so simple now when Herbie goes up to town, because he stays at his club. All the other delegates are stuck in these awful hotels, but he spends the night in comfort at Blake's."

"Very nice indeed."

"Oh yes. He meets such interesting people there, you know."

"I'm sure."

"The sort of people who he mixes with naturally. The sort of people he should have been mixing with all his life, but you know, the demands of the business have kept his social circle . . . parochial until now."

"And he'll be back tomorrow, will he?"

"Very late this evening."

They were silent. Charles looked out of the window. The view was magnificent, rolling hills shading away towards the distant mountains of Wales. The only building in sight was a huge square mansion about two miles away, set on a hill-top, dominating the entire landscape.

Velma Inchbald must have followed his gaze, because she identified the mansion. "Onscombe House. But you probably knew that."

"No, I didn't, actually."

"Willie Kitestone's place."

"Oh." He sensed that Velma wanted him to ask further about this familiarity. "You mean Lord Kitestone?" he asked, with a sufficiency of awe in his tone.

A smile irradiated her fat features. He had said the right thing. "Yes. Willie and Herbie are *such* good friends. You know, it's what I said about Herbie mixing with more interesting people. I mean, he hasn't got all the education and that, he's made his own way, but Herbie really is a member of Nature's aristocracy. He and Willie have such respect for each other. It was Willie who put him up for Blake's, you know.''

So that was one little mystery explained. ''Lord Kitestone's the Patron of the theatre, isn't he?'' asked Charles.

''Yes. That was one of Herbie's brainwaves. The Regent was being threatened at the time and Herbie thought, let's get the biggest name in the area on our side, so he wrote to Willie. That's really how they got to know each other.''

''Ah.''

''And they got on like a house on fire from the start. Oh, we're quite often invited up to Onscombe, you know.''

Charles made suitable impressed noises.

''Such a generous man, Willie. I mean, I don't think he's that well off... Well, obviously he is by our standards, but not for someone keeping up an establishment like that. No, I'm sure there were rumors some years back that he was going to have to sell Onscombe. But you'd never know it. He is such a generous entertainer. Do you know, he let us borrow his villa in Corsica last summer...?''

''Really?'' Had that been some sort of bribe, Charles wondered, though he couldn't for the life of him imagine why Lord Kitestone should want to bribe Herbie Inchbald. Some question of planning permission, perhaps?

But such speculation was dashed by Velma's next words. ''Of course, Herbie insisted we pay him rent. Never take anything for nothing, Herbie wouldn't. Sometimes I think he's *over*scrupulous about that sort of thing. But he always says to me, 'No, Velma, someone in my position can't be too careful. Local Councilors are constantly under public scrutiny, and even a simple little goodwill gesture can be easily misinterpreted. No, Velma, I never accept something for nothing.' ''

Years of living with him had enabled her so to take on her husband's intonations that it sounded as if Herbie himself was speaking.

Charles said, ''Good principle'' or some other vague cliché.

And then he noticed Frances standing in the doorway of the bar.

"Oh, er, Mrs. Inchbald, would you excuse me? My wife's arrived."

Velma shifted her bulk in the chair as if to suggest that Frances might come across and join them, but Charles, unworried by his rudeness, said, "No, I'm sorry, but I need to see her on her own."

"Oh, I'm sure I wasn't wanting to . . ."

"I haven't seen her for a long time," said Charles, as he walked across the room.

Somehow they both wanted to be outside, so before they had a drink, they took a turn around the hotel garden. This showed the same neglect as the rest of the premises. The straight lines of its formal design were shaggy with weeds. The gravel of the paths rose up in uneven hillocks. The white painted trellis of an arbor had collapsed in a tangle of lathes. Dandelions and plantain broke up the surface of the croquet lawn.

It was getting dark. They walked hand in hand. He could feel on her thumb the familiar scar a kitchen-knife had made once when they were together.

"I'm sorry I had to change the arrangement," Frances said rather formally. "About lunch. I thought I'd be free all day, but . . . something came up."

"David?" Charles was determined not to avoid the name.

She nodded. "I thought he'd be tied up with . . . his family all day, but then his wife got invited out to lunch and he was free and he expected me to be free, and I couldn't tell him where I was going and . . . God, it's so complicated."

"He doesn't know you're here now?"

She shook her head. "But I had to see you. Now it means I've got a three-hour drive back in the small hours. Never mind." She stopped and looked at him. "I am just so confused, Charles. I've never been in this situation before."

"You mean, having an affair with someone married?"

"Well, no, I haven't done that, I agree. I had no idea how complicated it was . . . all the times you can phone, times

you can't phone, meeting in places you won't meet anyone
you know...I don't know how people manage."

"They do. Always have."

She caught the additional meaning in his words and
grinned at him ruefully. "Of course. You know all about it,
Charles."

"Not all. A little. Maybe I should give you a few tips."

Frances laughed out loud. They put their arms around
each other and kissed.

"It's not just that that's complicated," Frances giggled.
"He also seems to be jealous of you..."

"I suppose that's flattering."

"Maybe. But it means I daren't even talk about you. And
then I start feeling guilty towards you—though God knows I
have no need to. And then...God, I don't know..." She
gestured at herself pitifully. "And see the result—one totally
mixed-up mess."

They looked into each other's eyes in the growing dusk.
Each saw pain, and confusion, and resignation, and a spark
of humor.

"Frances," Charles asked gently, "is he the real thing?"

"David?"

"Yes."

She looked away. "I don't know. Just don't know. When
it started, it was just so...unexpected. I was carried along.
Yes, it was wonderful, but sort of unreal. Then I started to
feel confused. Now...I don't know. So much of the relationship is intrigue, the times we spend together are so
rushed...we don't seem to be together for long enough to
judge whether it's actually working or not."

"A lot of affairs survive for a very long time on that sort
of excitement."

"Maybe. I'm not sure that my nerves are up to it."

It was odd talking to Frances about her having an affair.
He felt very close to her. The fact that there was another
man she slept with did not seem relevant. It was something
that he could appreciate intellectually, but not imaginatively.
It did not make any difference to the warmth there was
between them.

"Perhaps," he suggested sagely, "you should employ me as a consultant on how to conduct an illicit affair..."

"Why. Charles? What's your success-rate like?"

"Abysmal," he confessed.

And Frances laughed again, a clear relaxed laugh.

As the meal progressed, they both knew what was going to happen, but it was over coffee and Armagnac that Charles actually put it into words.

"I want you, Frances."

"I know. I want you too, Charles."

"I wouldn't recommend my digs. They are guarded by something that Hercules ought to have mopped up as one of his labors."

"Ah. So...?"

"They don't appear to be overbooked here. I'll go and see." Charles rose from the table. "What name shall I say—Mr. and Mrs. Smith?"

"You may joke, Charles, but I feel as if I'm doing something utterly criminal."

"Why? We are married."

"I know," said Frances. And it was not said in a tone of unqualified approval.

It was good. They needed each other, they knew each other, they wanted each other, and it was good.

Nothing was solved. Nothing was sorted out. Nothing was said about anything relevant, no plans, no intentions for the future, no discussion of what would happen to Frances and David, no demands that Charles would give up other women, nothing.

Nothing but their pleasure in being together at that moment.

Frances had to leave at five to make it back to town for a day's headmistressing. A night-porter (the adolescent from the bar the night before) was roused to let her out.

It was cold out on the gravel of the car park. Both felt tired and a little shocked by what had happened.

They stood by the yellow Renault. Frances' face looked drained as Charles kissed her, this time without passion.

"We'll see each other again," he murmured, as usual supplying no place, no date.

"Yes."

She sighed deeply and got into the car. She wound down the window and said to him without resentment, just as a statement of fact, "Thank you, Charles Paris. I think you've just ruined my life again."

And she drove back to London.

CHAPTER
SIXTEEN

"OF COURSE," GRUMBLED Mimi, "I've had gentlemen stay out all night before. Some been drunk, some been philandering. I know all about it. They tell Mimi."

She paused, waiting perhaps for Charles to pour out his confession. If so, she waited in vain.

"Because they know Mimi doesn't pass judgment. I accept human beings for what they are, warts and all. A lot of my gentlemen've brought back women here, knowing they're safe, knowing Mimi'll understand."

It was half-past ten and Charles had just got back. He had returned to bed at the Rugland Spa Hotel and woken again at nine, feeling more peaceful than for some weeks.

Under Mimi's relentless barrage, he would normally have gone straight out again. But he had given Gerald the number there and had a slight hope of hearing from the solicitor before eleven.

"I suppose you'll be wanting breakfast now." Mimi gathered her green candlewick about her, preparatory to rising. "Most of my gentlemen want a really big breakfast after the sort of night you've just had."

"No, thank you."

"Oh, they do. I remember when one of my gentlemen

was having an affair with the hairdresser in Raleigh
Street . . . Big secret it was, but he told Mimi, because he
knew I'd be discreet. Anyway, he'd be out all night and
come in so hungry you'd—''

"No, really thanks. I had a very good breakfast at the
Rugland Spa Hotel.''

"Rugland Spa Hotel,'' Mimi repeated, and Charles cursed
himself for giving her even the smallest solid fact. He knew
it would be filed away and provide anecdote-fodder to which
some other poor gentleman would be subjected.

"I've heard the Rugland Spa Hotel breakfasts are very
stingy.''

"No, it was fine.''

"Because it's a matter of moments for me to rustle up
some scrambled eggs for you.''

"No. Really.''

"I mean, there's nothing like home cooking.'' She made
it sound like an accusation.

"No.''

She subsided back into her folds of candlewick, and
looked at Charles with ill-disguised disapproval. "I'm surprised you haven't gone off to rehearsal yet.''

"Not called till later.'' He didn't want to go into all the
circumstances which had caused *Shove It*'s rehearsal schedule to be suspended. Though Mimi probably knew anyway.
"And also I'm vaguely expecting a phone call.''

"Oh.'' Mimi digested this information for a moment, and
then said casually, "Someone did ring for you just before
you come in.''

"Why on earth didn't you tell me?''

"I told him you was out on the razzle,'' she continued,
ignoring his question.

"Who was it?''

"Somebody Venables.''

Mimi said no, she didn't mind him using her phone, but it
was clear that her sitting there eavesdropping was part of the
deal. Still, if Gerald had an appointment at eleven, there
wasn't time to go anywhere else.

"Oh, morning, Charles," said the solicitor when he got through. "Gather you've been being a naughty boy again."

"Ha. Ha."

"Another nice little actress? Don't worry, I won't tell Frances—though I suppose we don't have to worry about that anymore."

Charles did not wish to pursue the ironies of that particular line of conversation and asked brusquely, "Did you get anything on Schlenter?"

"A bit. Nothing very criminal. Just basic background."

"I'd be glad to hear it. There might be something."

"Okay then. here's a quick history: Schlenter and Schlenter— two brothers, I think—started as ordinary estate agents in the sixties, North London . . . Highbury, Islington, that area. Did very well in the property boom of the late sixties, early seventies. Just residential then—you know, that was an area where a lot of the old terraces were being gentrified—old tenants died off, plenty of grants available to tart up the properties—there was a killing to be made and Schlenter and Schlenter were right in the middle of it. If you're looking for anything criminal, that's the time you should be concentrating on."

"What do you mean?"

"It was the hey-day of the 'winkler'. A lot of the property companies had them, to winkle out sitting tenants in premises they had bought."

"How did it work?"

"Variety of ways. Little old lady sitting in her little flat, feeling secure—smooth young man from estate agent comes around with check-book, offers her something to get out. Not much, but probably more money than most of the little old ladies had ever seen, so a few accepted. Those who didn't remained sitting in their little flats, feeling a little less secure. Next time maybe the smooth young man has a big growling Alsatian with him when he comes around. Or builders arrive saying the garden wall's not safe, needs replacing. They knock it down, cover the debris with a tatty tarpaulin and disappear for a few months. Or pipes get broken, or essential repairs don't get done. Usually the little old ladies reach some sort of breaking point and get out.''

"Leaving a property with vacant possession?''

"Exactly. Worth a great deal more money.''

"And the Schlenters were right into all that?''

Gerald Venables' professional caution stepped in. "No, I didn't say that. All I said was that a lot of that sort of thing went on in the area where Schlenter and Schlenter had their operation.''

"Okay.''

"And it's not the sort of allegation to flash around carelessly. They are now extremely respectable and quick on the draw with writs.''

"I will be very circumspect. How did they become so respectable?''

"That started around 1970. They were coining it from the residential property and starting to buy up other local estate agents . . . Ringling and Sons, Spielberg, Pugh and Fosco, Dutters . . . and a few more. Then they incorporated the lot into Schlenter Estates and started to diversify into bigger projects . . . you know, hotels, town center developments, that sort of scale . . .''

"Any evidence of corruption?''

"Oh, I'm sure all the usual things went on. A few local councilors suddenly might appear with new cars, the odd inconvenient building might burn down, small stores might find they were having difficulty getting their deliveries through . . . But all very discreet, nothing you could ever make stick. Just normal business practice, if you like.''

"Where were their town center developments?''

"All over. Good few in Wales, traditionally the center of local council corruption. But they weren't just operating in England. Expanding abroad during those boom years . . . Africa, Australia, Hong Kong, even further afield. God,'' said Gerald with wistful respect, "they must have made a lot of money.''

"Then what happened?''

"Well, the property boom really peaked in '72. Then whatever you did made money. But the crash came, inevitably. '74, '75 were probably the worst. A lot of people got their fingers burned. A lot of property companies went out of business. Schlenter Estates were particularly vulnerable. They'd expanded so quickly, they'd got all these developments stretched all over the world, and suddenly there wasn't any money to be made in property."

"But they didn't fold. They're still around."

"Yes. But they very nearly went under. Around 1975 I think both of the original Schlenters died, and it looked like the end. But then they got taken over."

"By Fowler Rose Stillman?"

"Ye-es, but not directly. They were actually absorbed by Clarton Investments, which is a subsidiary of FRS."

"Oh, I see. But Fowler Rose Stillman is the top of the pyramid?"

"By no means. Everything, it seems, is owned by someone else. The average member of the public would have a fit if it was actually spelled out to them how few companies own almost everything in this country. No, Fowler Rose Stillman was taken over a couple of years back by Polycopius . . ."

"The hotel chain?"

"Hotels, television, record companies, films, you name it. Anyway, Polycopius merged eighteen months ago with Carker Glyde Securities."

"So Schlenter Estates are actually owned by Carker Glyde?"

"Yes. Or were at the end of trading on Friday. And you can't get more respectable than that. Long established in the City, high international reputation, half the House of Lords on their Board . . ."

"Really? Like who?"

"What, you want their names?" asked Gerald in bewilderment.

"If you've got them."

"Just a sec. I've got their annual report somewhere. Ah, here we are. And you want me to read out the list of directors?"

"Please."

Charles could visualize his friend shrugging as he began to read. But the actor felt insanely confident, and when the name came up, he asked Gerald to stop and repeat it.

"Lord Kitestone."

"Thank you. And you say the take-over was eighteen months ago?"

"Give or take a month."

"Thank you very much."

"Charles, what are you on about?" But before he could be answered, Gerald was interrupted, apparently by someone entering his office. "What, Polly? Oh yes. Great. Send him in. Listen, Charles, Bill Walsingham's arrived, so I'm going to have to find out the rest later."

"That's fine. I've got what I wanted. I'll—"

"Bill, how are you? Great to see you! How was Australia? Just a sec, Talk later, Charles. Okay?"

"Fine. 'Bye, Gerald. And thank you."

Inchbald Haulage Co. was a little way out of Rugland Spa on the London Road. The main gates opened on to a large yard, in which three yellow articulated lorries boasted their owner's name in red letters. The office was a low cedar-clad one-story building with a lot of windows. The secretary's room was animated with displays of plastic flowers. Everything was neat and tidy, reflecting a well-run and probably profitable business, but it was not the setting in which one expected to find a member of Blake's Club.

"My name's Charles Paris. To see Mr. Inchbald. I rang earlier."

"Yes, of course. Mr. Inchbald, Mr. Paris has arrived," she breathed into the intercom.

"Send him in!"

Herbie Inchbald's office was as neat and prosperous as the rest of the outfit. Its furniture was low and Scandinavian. On the walls fluorescent paintings on black velvet and framed cars made of clock-parts once again made Charles wonder about the Councilor's artistic standards.

"Come in, Mr. Paris. Sit down. Would you care for a coffee?"

"No, thank you." Charles thought the confrontation might become ugly, and didn't want to start it on too cozy a level.

"When you rang, you said it was something about Tony Wensleigh's death."

"Yes."

"Terrible tragedy, that."

"It was. But it's just one in a sequence of things that have been going wrong at the Regent."

"What, you mean Gordon Tremlett's accident? Oh, I wouldn't call that a sequence."

"Not just that. I mean, the way the artistic standards had been slipping."

"Did you really think they were?" The little man ran his fingers through his mane of hair as he reflected on this idea. "Well, maybe Tony was getting a bit past it. Perhaps, though it's an awful way for it to happen, having to bring in a new man may be the saving of the the-ettah."

"I wonder whether the theatre *can* still be saved."

Herbie Inchbald looked very affronted. "What on earth do you mean?"

Charles stared straight at him. "It's my belief that someone very closely connected with the theatre has actually been trying to sabotage it, to ensure that it's in such a bad state when the Maugham Cross development is next discussed that nobody will be able to argue persuasively enough to save it."

"That's a rather extreme allegation, Mr. Paris."

Charles shrugged. "Maybe, but I think it is the case. I think Tony knew too, and I think it was fighting against the pressure of that sabotage that drove him to suicide."

"But who would possibly want the theatre to close?"

"Schlenter Estates would, for a start."

"Yes, obviously, but—"

"I wouldn't think it would be long before they come in with another offer for the whole Maugham Cross site."

Herbie Inchbald colored. "Well, er..."

"You mean they already have?"

He nodded. "Just heard this morning. Bigger offer, quite a bit bigger." He looked miserable.

"Quick off the mark. They're shrewd operators. And what kind of luck do you think you'll have this time persuading the Council that the Regent is a hyper-efficient bastion of culture that must be preserved at all costs? What have we had in the last three weeks—disastrous production of a disastrous play, public demonstration about the next production, one near-fatal accident and the suicide of the Artistic Director under something of a cloud over his handling of the theatre's funds? What do you reckon your chances are this time, Mr. Inchbald?"

The head sagged forward, "Low," came the reply. "Very low."

"Okay, it could just be a sequence of bad luck. I think there's more to it. I think it's been organized."

"But who by?" The Councilor now looked shifty, cornered.

"Ultimately by Schlenter Estates, but I think a few other people have been used on the way. People who are not above bribery."

The Councilor bridled. "If that remark's aimed at me. I'd advise you to withdraw it. I have never accepted a bribe in my life. Schlenter tried it on with me, I don't deny it. They made some very attractive offers to me—cars, holiday homes, you name it. But I am proud to say I turned down every one of them. I'm not the kind of man to be bought that way."

"No. I agree. Not that way."

"I resent your tone, Mr. Paris."

"You wouldn't be bought by a direct offer or a gift, nor by any material inducement. No, somebody who wanted to buy you would have to appeal to your snobbery."

Herbie Inchbald rose from his seat to his full height, which wasn't very high. "Get out of my office!"

"Not yet. I want to ask you about your friendship with Lord Kitestone."

"What of it?"

"You've seen a lot of him in the last few years."

"So what? Who the devil do you think you are—asking me about my friendships? Lord Kitestone has been a friend since I asked him to be Patron of the Regent. We hit it off very well together, as it happens.''

"And you were great friends right from the start, right from when you asked him to be Patron?''

''Well, no, we took a bit of time to get to know each other. And he was very tied up at the time, problems with the estate and that, thought he was going to have to sell up, in fact. But in the last year or so, we've seen a lot more of each other, built up a great deal of mutual respect..."

"In the last eighteen months?''

"Yes."

"So much so that he's allowed you to use his holiday home in Corsica.''

This again caught the Councilor on the raw. "Don't try it, Mr. Paris. I paid him rent for that villa, and I can prove it.''

"I know. Are you aware who owns Schlenter Estates, Mr. Inchbald?''

"I assumed they were independent. Well, perhaps they're part of some conglomerate...I don't know." It was hard to tell whether this hesitant answer was the truth, or whether the Councilor was bluffing.

"Let me outline a little story for you, Mr. Inchbald. Fiction, of course, but maybe you'll find something relevant in it. Let's say we have a peer of the realm with a large estate to maintain and he's feeling the pinch...His income just isn't big enough to cope with it all. True, he's got a few directorships which bring in a bit of loot for no effort, but it's not sufficient money. And then let's say one of the companies of which he's director takes over, through a fairly lengthy chain of ownership, a property company. Normally, it wouldn't interest him much, but in this case he does become involved. Someone in the property company comes to him with a proposal...a new mortgage, a loan maybe, something anyway that will let him off the hook financially...

"Sounds good, says the noble lord, adding cautiously, is there anything I have to do in return? Yes, the property company replies soothingly, but it's something very small.

All we want you to do is to get chummy with a local councilor in your area and—''

"I've heard enough of this!" snapped Herbie Inchbald. "It's slander and I will see to it that—"

"As I said," Charles overrode him, "it's only a story. To make it even begin to be slanderous, you'd have to fill in some of the names. Call the peer of the realm Lord Kitestone, for example . . . Call the company of which he's a director Carker Glyde Securities . . . Call the property company they took over eighteen months ago Schlenter Estates . . . Call the Councilor—"

"Stop." Herbie Inchbald's face was ashen. "is he really a director of the company that owns Schlenter?"

"Yes. You can check it. What's that very useful book called—'Who Owns Who'?"

"Oh, my God." This time the Councillor did not appear to be acting. His shock at the revelation was quite genuine.

"So, to complete my little story, all I need to know is what the noble lord was delegated to get from the Councilor. What was the little favor? I think I know what the Councilor got in return."

Inchbald picked himself up and returned aggressively to the fray. "You're on a hiding to nothing, Paris. I've never accepted a bribe from anyone, and certainly not from Lord Kitestone. You can check my bank accounts, search my house if you like. You won't find anything."

"I'm not talking about anything as crude as money. As I said, it had to be something that appealed to your snobbery . . . something that the noble lord could give at no cost to himself, but something that you could not get from any other source."

"I don't follow you."

"No? I am right, am I not, in saying that Lord Kitestone put you up for Blake's Club?"

"Yes, but . . ." The Councilor looked very angry again. "That was just a friendly gesture on his part, because we got on so well. Good God, can't friends do each other favors nowadays without everyone getting suspicious?"

"Of course they can. And what favor did you do him in return?"

"Nothing. Well, I mean, hardly anything. He just gave me some advice and I took it. Wasn't even a favor to him, as it happened. Favor to someone else, another example of Willie's generosity. Turned out to be a favor to me too, as things worked out."

"But, nonetheless, he didn't put you up for the club until you'd agreed to accept his advice?"

"God, you make it sound so cold-blooded. It was just two friends helping each other out, that's all."

"You scratch my back . . ."

"Exactly . . ."

"Okay, I know how Lord Kitestone scratched your back. How did you scratch his?"

"It was nothing. It was just . . ."

And Herbie Inchbald told him.

As he finished, he smiled weakly and said. "And if you can find any corruption in that, good luck to you. It's been a positive benefit to the theatre, and without Lord Kitestone it wouldn't have happened. I think you're barking up the wrong tree with all your talk of sabotage, Mr. Paris. You certainly are if you're trying to point the finger at me." Herbie Inchbald sat down and tried to regain some composure behind his desk. "I am a devoted supporter of the Regent Theatre. And so is Willie Kitestone."

Charles gave the Councilor the benefit of the doubt and believed his first assertion.

But not the second.

CHAPTER
SEVENTEEN

CHARLES' MIND WAS now working well. He hadn't slept much the night before, but the tiredness heightened his efficiency rather than diminished it. He was on a high, feeling good, and his mind responded, making sudden new connections in the case.

After his interview with Herbie Inchbald he returned to Mimi's and, ignoring her curiosity as to what he was doing there at that time of day, went straight up to his bedroom. There he got out the file Martha Wensleigh had given him and took another look at its contents.

The brainwave came quickly. He looked at his watch. Quarter to one. Might just make it. Clutching some of the papers in his hand, he ran downstairs to the telephone and, oblivious of Mimi's eavesdropping, dialed.

"Gerald."

"Charles? Look, this is rather inconvenient. I said—"

"I know. You're just about to go out for a long, good lunch. Where?"

"Langan's, as it happens."

"Of course. Well, you can spare me two minutes. Listen, is Bill still with you?"

"Right beside me."

"Put him on. I want a word."

"Very well, but..."

"Hello?"

"Bill, hi. This is Charles Paris."

"Oh. Good to hear you. What can I—"

"I want to pick your brains."

"You're welcome to anything you can find there."

"Right. You've just come back from Australia, where you've been directing...?"

"For the last five years, yeah."

"So you know the theatrical scene out there pretty well?"

"Such as it is. Yes, I guess I do."

"Right." Charles consulted the sheets in his hand. "Do you know the Theatre Royal, Adelaide?"

"Sure. Nice old building."

"And the Artistic Director, Ralph Johnson."

"Ralph who?"

"Johnson."

"Never heard of him."

"This'd be back in 1975."

"Before my time. I'd have thought I'd have heard the name, though."

"Okay. Try another. The Dominion, Perth?"

"Know it well."

"Artistic Director, Rich Coleman?"

"Never heard of him. Jed Spencer had the job all the time I was out there."

"What about the Hippodrome, Melbourne?"

"Know that too."

"And the Artistic Director there in '79 was...?"

"Bruce Wade."

"Not Greg Avon?"

"Never heard the name. What is this—a *Mastermind* special subject on the theatres of Australia?"

"No. I will explain. I haven't got time at the moment. There's only one more. Do you know the Kelly Theatre in Sydney?"

"Should do."

"And you're going to tell me the Artistic Director there last year was not Jim Vaslis."

"That one, Charles, I can confirm without a shadow of a doubt. For the last five years *I* have been Artistic Director of the Kelly Theatre in Sydney. That's the job I've just finished."

Charles sighed with relief. "Thank you very much, Bill."

"No problem. I wish I knew what the hell it was about."

"One day, Bill, over a very long and very drunken lunch, I will tell you."

"I look forward to that, Charles."

"Could you put me back to Gerald, just for a sec?"

"Okay."

"Gerald, listen, have you got a copy of *The British Theatre Directory* there?" The solicitor grunted assent. "Could you look up the Pavilion Theatre, Darlington, for me?"

"Okay. Just a sec. I wish you'd explain, Charles."

"If I did it might make you late for your lunch."

"Oh, that's true. Some other time then. Right . . . the Pavilion, you said. It's owned by . . . ah, the site was bought up quite recently."

"By whom, Gerald?"

"Schlenter Estates. Is that significant?"

"Yes, Gerald. It is."

So all the references were quite meaningless. The Australian ones were forged, and the Darlington one presumably dictated by Schlenter Estates. No, more likely it was genuine. After all, that one could be checked easily, and Donald Mason must have spent some time finding out about theatre administration. Six months as Assistant Front of House Manager at Darlington would have given enough background to someone with a genuine flair for organization. And Schlenter had presumably arranged for him to take the job.

They had also assumed, correctly, that the average provincial rep theater would know nothing about the Australian scene, and be too mean to ring up the other side of the world to check the references.

Charles now knew that Donald Mason's career *hadn't* been, and, his memory working well, thought he might be able to find out what it *had* been.

The old lady was in her usual niche in the pub behind the theatre and accepted another bottle of Guinness gratefully.

"I *do* know you," she said. "Seen you before, you know."

"In here. Just the once."

"That's right," she said, raising his hopes that she would prove to be a reliable witness. "Your name's Lionel," she continued, dashing them.

"Charles."

"That's right, Charles." She nodded her head, which seemed loose on her shoulders. "Charles, I knew another Charles once. Had this nasty habit in the park. He used to—"

Charles didn't want to get too involved in irrelevant reminiscence, so he nudged the conversation on by asking, "Was this in Islington?"

"Around the Angel, yes."

"Where you used to live?"

"That's right, yes. Don't live there no more. Had this nice little flat. Now I live with my daughter. She wouldn't let me go to the Old People', not my daughter. She's got this bird, my daughter has. Canary, it is. I don't care for canaries . . ."

Once again Charles had to stop the conversation from straying too far off course.

"Your flat was in Blenley Terrace, wasn't it? he asked, memory working overtime.

"Blenley Terrace, that's right." Again she started the unnerving nodding. "Nice place it was, around there. Nice people, like a village. Not now. All been tarted up now."

"Yes. Listen, I want you to try to remember something."

"You come to the right person." She stopped nodding and fixed her faded eyes on him seriously. "I got one of them photographic memories. Never forget a face. Nor a name, Lionel."

"Charles."

"That's right. Charles."

"Listen, when I last came in here, week or so ago, someone else came in, someone you said you recognized from Islington . . ."

She looked at him blankly. Her mouth sagged. Charles feared he had hoped for too much. Her mind had really gone.

"Man about thirty. Tall, pin-striped suit. Blond hair."

Something in his description struck a chord in her memory, because her expression changed suddenly. "Oh, I remember *him*," she spat out venomously. "He was why I left my flat."

"What do you mean?"

"He said he come from the estate agents. Offered me money to move out. But I didn't want to. I liked it there. All my friends there. Didn't care how much money, I told him. I didn't want to move. He kept coming back and I kept saying no. Then he started coming strange times, very late at night, six in the morning. But I still said no.

"Then I didn't see him no more, but . . . things started happening."

"What sort of things?" Charles asked softly.

"Be knocking on my door in the middle of the night. Then someone banged a brick through my window. Plumbing started going funny. Bath overflowed and soaked the people downstairs. I never left it on, I know, but they got in the social worker. And then there was the gas."

"Gas?"

"Yes. Gas was left on all my rings. Nearly a big explosion. They said I wasn't safe living on my own. But I ask you, would I leave all of them on? Anyone could leave one on by mistake, but not all of them." She sniffed. "Anyway, the social worker got on to my daughter and she come, and the social worker said I couldn't manage alone, and I'd have to go to the Old People's. And my daughter, bless her, says no, and brought me up here."

"So you never went back to the flat?"

"No."

"And you think the man you saw in here was behind it?"

"Bloody sure. I remember, the estate agents was called Spielberg, Pugh and Fosco. And his name was Mr. Mason."

Charles bought the old lady another Guinness. She had earned it.

As he stood at the bar, he pieced it together. So Donald Mason had started out as a "winkler" for one of the estate agents the Schlenters took over. Then he probably had gone to Australia as the property company expanded in the early 1970s. Back to England, brief spell in Darlington to learn the new business, then, with Lord Kitestone leaning discreetly on Herbie Inchbald, he got the Rugland Spa job. Winkling again.

Just the same, but on a larger scale. Instead of getting rid of one old lady to clear a house, his job was to get rid of a theatre to clear a town center site for development.

He was going to have to go and talk to Donald Mason.

He ordered himself a large Bell's as a bracer.

CHAPTER
__EIGHTEEN__

LESLIE BLATT WAS coming out of the administrative office as Charles reached the top of the stairs. The elderly playwright looked extremely pleased with himself.

"Hello, Charles," he said, rubbing his hands together. "We're going to be working together."

"What do you mean?"

"Donald's just asked me and I've said yes. It's a few years since I've done it, but I'm sure I'll manage. It's a real challenge."

"What are you talking about?"

"*Shove It*. Donald's just asked me to take over as director."

"What!"

"Well, don't sound like that. I used to direct, you know. Still got a lot of ideas, and I've been following most of the rehearsals. I'd really like to get my hands on a play like this."

Not just on the play, either. Charles visualized the chaos that would be caused among the naked actresses by Leslie Blatt's wandering hands as he "directed" them.

"Well, aren't you going to congratulate me, Charles?"

"What? Oh yes. Congratulations."

"We're hoping to get ready for an opening on Friday. Only two days late."

"I see."

"Rehearsal ten sharp tomorrow morning. See you then."

The old goat pranced downstairs, chuckling to himself.

Charles knocked on the office door, and was bidden to enter.

Donald Mason sat behind his desk, every bit the smart executive in another pin-striped suit. Too smart, really, for the theatre. Charles felt he should have smelt a rat earlier. But no, he—presumably like everyone else—had been just relieved to see someone who appeared to be efficient in the role of General Manager.

"Charles. What can I do for you?"

"I just met Leslie. Gather he's going to take over directing *Shove It*."

"That's right. Seems ideal. Difficult to get in someone from outside at this stage, and at least he's been following the production."

"He'd follow anything where he knew women were going to take their clothes off."

Donald Mason looked up sharply, surprised by Charles' change of tone. "Have you been drinking?"

"The actor shook his head. "Not enough to affect my judgment."

"Oh. Well, Leslie is going to be directing. I've made the decision."

"Yes. I'm sure you have. Yet another in a skillfully composed sequence of wrong decisions."

The General Manager was stung by this. "What are you talking about?"

"I think it was almost a compliment, Donald. You've managed the whole thing very well. Constantly talking about the importance of right decisions and ensuring that the wrong ones are made. Constantly stressing the need for company loyalty and spreading divisive rumors behind people's backs. Constantly saying how much you want the Regent to survive and all the time undermining it."

"Are you going to explain what you're talking about, or do I have to listen to more of this abusive rhetoric?"

"I'll explain." Charles took a deep breath. "I've blown your cover, Donald."

"What does that mean?"

"I know that all the references you produced to get this job were forgeries. I know that you never worked in the theater in Australia. I know that you started working for an estate agency called Spielberg, Pugh and Fosco and I reckon that you're still in the pay of Schlenter Estates!"

There was a silence. Charles tensed. He didn't know what to expect after his outburst, but was ready for some form of physical assault.

To his amazement, he heard Donald Mason laughing. "Very good, Charles, very good. I heard you had a bit of a reputation as a detective, and I'm most impressed by this demonstration of your skill."

With the wind momentarily taken out of his sails, Charles blustered. "Do you deny that you were put into this job to bring the theatre to its knees?"

"No, I don't."

"Pretty easy, too, wasn't it? You could run circles around Tony Wensleigh. So vague he was, so abstracted, so trusting . . . Always out at a rehearsal, so that you could do what you liked here. Spread rumors about his inefficiency, libel him—always with an expression of deep regret that you had to do it.

"The sabotage went deep. The choice of plays . . . you contrived that very well. You knew Herbie was totally ignorant about art, and you knew Leslie would agree with anything so long as his dire little thriller was included. So you lumbered Tony with this awful program, and then had the nerve to tell everyone that he had chosen them, and that his judgment was going . . ."

Donald Mason shrugged. "Yes," he said with an air of indifference.

"You're not making any attempt to deny it."

"Why should I? it's all true."

"But . . ." Charles found himself blustering again. It was

like trying to get satisfaction out of punching a sponge. "I mean, the way you played us all along, making us believe you were the long-suffering one, constantly clearing up after Tony. Little calculated touches of humanity—like when you didn't sack me, like when you offered me the part in *Shove It* . . ."

Donald smiled with something approaching insolence. "Yes. Of course that was not just magnanimity."

"What do you mean?"

"I thought keeping a piss-artist like you around in the company was another good method of disruption."

"Good God." Charles was almost lost for words. He found himself getting angry. This was not at all how he had intended the interview to turn out. "So that's why you went against Tony's advice and kept me on."

"Oh, I didn't go against Tony's advice. He wanted to give you a second chance."

"But you said . . ."

"Yes. And you believed me. I've often been told that one of my great strengths is my plausibility."

"But . . . but how can you be so bloody cool about it all?"

"Why shouldn't I be cool? I was put into this job to see that the theatre closed within a year, and I reckon I've pretty well achieved that."

"But what's going to happen when I expose you?"

"Expose what? Have you proof of any crime that I've committed?"

"Well . . . That accident to Gordon Tremlett—I bet you were behind that."

"Proof I said, Charles, proof. Even if I did fix it—and I'm not saying I did, in case you have some tape recorder hidden away—how could you prove it?"

"Well . . ." Charles felt momentarily lost. "What about Tony? You hounded him so much, confused him, accused him . . . you drove him to kill himself."

The General Manager smiled again, infuriatingly. "That I think you'd find even more difficult to prove, Charles."

The actor gaped.

"You see, it's so easy to fool people. They set themselves up. They want to be conned. I mean, someone like Tony was just a sitting target. So trusting, as you said. So incapable of fighting back, assuming he could ever identify his enemy. Ultimately so stupid."

"But there have been crimes committed!" Charles insisted, rising involuntarily from his chair with fists clenched.

Donald gave him a cool appraisal. "If you were to hit me, that would be a crime. And I would see that you were charged with it."

Charles subsided, trying to calm himself. Slow down, slow down, stick to the one crime he could prove. "What about those forged references? Those are real enough. They're proof against you."

"Okay." The General Manager still refused to be ruffled. "So what would that be—a charge of False Pretenses, maybe? Might get a few months for that, I suppose . . ."

"Yes," said Charles, with a hardly adequate feeling of minor triumph.

"If, of course, you could find anyone to charge me . . ."

"What?"

"Listen. As you have so cleverly worked out, I was infiltrated here to put this theatre out of business. I think I've done pretty well. With this new offer coming in from Schlenter, with *Shove It* causing public demonstrations, with the Artistic Director committing suicide under a cloud, the whole set-up looks pretty shaky. Not a great deal of faith around Rugland Spa in the Regent's management. Do you think that that faith would be increased by the revelation that that very management appointed as their General Manager someone with forged references?"

Slowly Charles let this sink in, and felt the full crushing power of its logic. The one charge that could be proven against Donald Mason would never be brought.

CHAPTER
NINETEEN

THE FRUSTRATION WAS total. It was even more frustrating than when he couldn't make sense of the case. Now he could, now he had arrived at the truth, only to find that truth brought no resolution. It was like chatting up an apparently avid girl all evening only to have her favors abruptly denied.

Charles fumed, because he knew Donald was right. He had been planted to bring down the theatre and the revelation of the subterfuge would only hasten its collapse. If there were someone strong around to handle the exposure it might work, but there wasn't. Tony had found the pressure too much and was no longer available. And Councilor Inchbald wasn't going to publicize the way he had been manipulated by his "friend," Lord Kitestone.

If there were something else, some actual crime that could be proved against Donald Mason. He had as good as admitted to engineering Gordon Tremlett's accident, but in the full confidence that no proof could ever be produced. Maybe he had also been responsible for the stabbing Charles had so narrowly escaped. It didn't seem in character, too rash an action for someone who planned so cold-bloodedly, but it was possible Donald had arranged it as another

random act of sabotage, another incident to get the anti-
theater councilors baying for enquiries.

But, even if that had been the case, evidence of Donald's
implication remained as elusive for the stabbing as for the
hanging.

Charles' fury was increased by the General Manager's
arrogant confidence. He had taken the job knowing that it
would end in collapse and presumably had some fatly paid
post lined up with Schlenter Estates for when he finally left
it. And he had done what was required very efficiently,
without a moment's hesitation on moral grounds. Driving
Tony Wensleigh to suicide was clearly a feat he regarded as
a major professional coup, not an action affecting the life of
a fellow human being.

Tony, Donald had said, had been stupid. Stupid for
showing normal human qualities like trust, stupid for giving
people the benefit of the doubt, stupid for letting the
pressure get to him.

No doubt Donald would apply the same adjective to
Charles. Everyone in the world was stupid to Donald,
because he knew he could run circles around any of them. A
person with no moral sense at all is capable of much greater
efficiency than those trammelled by doubt and benevolence.

And Charles could see no way of unsettling Donald
Mason's evil complacency.

He stumped round the now-hateful streets of Rugland
Spa, waiting for the pubs to open.

On the dot of five-thirty he went into the one behind the
theatre. He had vague thoughts of seeing the old lady again,
asking her more about the young winkler who had made her
life a misery. He didn't know what he hoped to find out. It
was all so long ago. To prove criminality at such a distance
and after so long would be virtually impossible.

Anyway, the old lady hadn't appeared, so the idea was
academic. Charles settled down to an evening of heavy
drinking which might, in time, induce oblivion. He didn't
drink beer; he went straight on to the Bell's.

So the wheel of his Rugland Spa drinking had come full

circle. It had started badly, even to the extent of his being hopelessly drunk on stage; then he had reformed; and here he was deliberately going back to the bad ways.

Then came the unwelcome thought of what had started him drinking the first time. Frances. Frances and her announcement of her new lover. He was still shocked by how much that had affected him.

But the previous night he had seen her, had spent with her. The confrontations of the day had pushed that to the back of his mind. But it had been good. They had so much together. He couldn't just let her slip out of his life.

In his increasingly maudlin state he made various resolutions. He must get Frances back. David he dismissed as an irrelevancy. Surely, if he really asked her to, Frances would come back to him, permanently. Of course, he'd have to reform, he knew that. Moderate the drinking, though that wasn't what really annoyed Frances; she had always been pretty tolerant about that. No, it was other women. She really didn't like him being unfaithful. And he had always found it hard to resist the appeal of a young actress. That had been the root of the trouble, that and the long separations caused by his work.

But he was fifty-five now and his prospects with young actresses waned further with each passing day. No more, he decided virtuously. Concentrate on Frances. Concentrate on getting Frances back. She was the only woman who really mattered to him, she was the only one who could cope with his low moods. He needed her.

"Charles Paris, isn't it?"

A Welsh voice broke into his earnest resolutions.

"Yes." He looked up into Frank Walby's bibulous baby face. "Hello. Can I get you a drink?"

He spoke with enthusiasm. Having taken the decision to get drunk, he knew it would be more pleasant to have a companion in his excesses, and also knew that Frank Walby was probably the most suitable candidate for that role in all of Rugland Spa.

The journalist accepted the offer with equal enthusiasm, specifying "a pint of Old and Filthy—they'll know what you mean."

Charles got himself another large Bell's and the two sat down and toasted each other.

Frank Walby emitted a long, lugubrious sigh. "Who was it who described his life as a long disease?"

"Alexander Pope, I think."

The journalist nodded. "Sounds right. And somebody else said it was incurable."

"That, I happen to know, was Abraham Cowley."

Frank Walby mimed clapping. "Oh, go to the top of the class, that boy. Very good."

"I seem to have a knack of remembering depressing quotations."

"Oh, you should do a book of them. I can see it—*The Oxford Book of Depressing Quotations*, edited by Charles Paris. 'Ideal bedside reading for all would-be suicides.' Sell like hot cakes, that would."

Charles grinned. Maybe the evening wouldn't turn out so badly after all.

"You've heard you'll have to wait a bit to review *Shove It*?"

"Yes. Friday, isn't it?"

"Uhuh. Should be. Are you going to do another of your swinging notices?"

"I'm not sure. I don't know that the last one really did the theatre much good. And, God knows, it needs all the help it can get at the moment."

"Yes." With his new knowledge of Donald Mason, Charles now realized that the appeal for Walby to judge the Regent's productions more rigidly was just another cynical device to weaken the theatre further. "No, I think you should go back to your old cozy style."

"You might be right. Will I like *Shove It*?"

"Well, don't let me prejudice you in any way, but I think you'll hate every minute of it."

"Oh dear." Walby groaned. "I can imagine exactly what I'll write . . . 'the bold decision to stage that controversial play, *Shove It*, was fully justified at the Regent Theatre last night. A splendid cast did more than justice to . . .' Pap, pap, pap . . ."

"But generous to an ailing institution."

"Yes. And at least it won't get me any threatening letters."

"Why? Did the last one?"

"Oh yes. Didn't I show you this?" He pulled a crumpled letter out of an equally crumpled jacket and handed it over.

Charles skimmed the contents ". . . filthy abuse of my work . . . showing your own total ignorance of the theatre . . . not the sort of thing I take lightly. . . would advise you to be careful walking around after dark . . . not the first time I've had to defend myself from bastards who attack my work . . ." He looked up. "It's not signed."

"No, but it's obvious who it came from, isn't it?"

"Leslie Blatt?"

"Yes." Walby chuckled. "Out to murder me—and presumably anyone else who disparages his magnum opus."

Charles stared. His mind was racing. "He hasn't made any attack on you?"

"No," Walby replied with a grin. "I wait in fear and trembling."

"Maybe you should," said Charles slowly.

He pieced it together. Perhaps there were two parallel but unconnected sequences of crimes. The crimes against the theatre, perpetrated by Schlenter Estates' cuckoo in the nest. And crimes against individuals, perpetrated by a crazed failed writer.

First, the stabbing . . . Leslie Blatt had thought "young Mr. Smartypants" was in the cupboard. And Rick Harmer had constantly derided the quality of *The Message Is Murder*.

Then the hanging . . . Gordon Tremlett, in his unthinking way, had spoken to the author of his "rubbishy old play."

And Antony Wensleigh, in his letter to Leslie Blatt, had said what he thought of it in no uncertain terms. And Antony Wensleigh had died.

For the first time, Charles wondered whether it really had been suicide.

Frank Walby was looking at him, rather puzzled by his silence.

"Frank, total change of subject—Tony's death . . ."

"Yes. What about it?"

"You covered it for the press, didn't you?"

"Yes. Even made the nationals—just."

"You think it was for real, don't you?"

"What do you mean?"

"That it really was suicide?"

"Oh, you want it to be a murder, do you?" The journalist chuckled. "High drama that would be, wouldn't it? No, I'm sorry, Charles. It was obviously intentional. He left this note. The police showed it to me."

"Who was it addressed to?"

"Nothing written on the envelope. Just an ordinary Regent Theatre one."

"Can you remember the exact wording?"

"Don't know, but I wrote it down."

The crumpled jacket yielded an equally crumpled shorthand notebook. Frank found the place and handed the book over.

The words Charles read he had seen before.

"SORRY ABOUT THE TOTAL COCK-UP OF EVERYTHING. NO EXCUSES. YOURS ABJECTEDLY, TONY."

Charles rushed into the theatre. His mind had done a complete U-turn, but was picking up speed in its new direction.

He was no longer thinking of Tony's apparent suicide as the work of Leslie Blatt. His suspicion had returned firmly to Donald Mason.

The coincidence was too great. Tony wouldn't have couched his suicide note in exactly the same words as his apology of the rehearsal room booking mix-up, though to someone who had not seen the letter in its original context, it could well read that way. Donald Mason had recognized that ambivalence and its potential future value when he had pocketed the note. And forgotten that Charles Paris had witnessed his action.

Nella Lewis was in the Green Room, sorting through some *Shove It* props. She looked mournful, bereft of Laurie Tichbourne and knowing that she was pretty unlikely ever to see him again. But Charles had no time for chat and sympathy. He just waved and went on stage to the ladder to the gallery.

He tried to remember exactly what Tony Wensleigh had

said on the evening he died. He had been manic, nearly hysterical, but certain points had emerged both in his conversation with Charles and in his phone-call to his wife.

One was that he reckoned he definitely had an enemy within the Regent Theatre set-up. Charles could now confidently identify that person as Donald Mason.

The second point was that, after a long period of confusion, Tony implied that he had at last made some breakthrough, perhaps found actual proof of his enemy's malpractices.

Third, he intended to confront his enemy. And, perhaps already suspicious of his opponent's ruthlessness after the accident to Gordon Tremlett, he wanted to have the gun with him when he made the confrontation.

Charles had rushed out of the props store when Tony fired at him (a firing he now felt sure had been unintentional). Tony hadn't followed him, but had locked the back door and gone out at the front into the administrative office. Before the details of the suicide came out, Charles had assumed that the Artistic Director had gone to confront his General Manager.

Suppose, after all, that was what had happened. Tony had bearded Donald in his office and presented him with evidence of his misdoings. An argument had developed, in the course of which Donald had got hold of the gun and shot his accuser. He then arranged the scene to look like suicide, put the note he had kept in the drawer, and went backstage.

He would have had plenty of time to do this before Charles arrived. And, while the actor had gone the long way, around the outside of the theatre, Donald could have cut through either the props store or the Wardrobe store. (In fact, Charles reasoned, if he had taken the latter course, he could almost guarantee not to be seen. It would have been toward the end of Act Two, when almost all of the stage staff were busy arranging the hanging of Colonel Fripp, and all of the rest of the cast were on stage.) Donald could then sit in the Green Room with a paper, which was how Charles found him when he broke the news of Tony's death, and give the impression he had been there for hours.

But what was the evidence that Tony had produced which

so threatened Donald? Perhaps he had found out the Schlenter connection and intended to reveal it at the Extraordinary Board Meeting of the following evening. Though Donald was unworried by exposure after Tony was dead, an attack from the living Artistic Director might ruin his plans and build up sympathy for the Regent's plight.

Whatever it was, Charles felt convinced that the key to the secret lay in the props store.

He opened the door and switched on the light. The nearer bulb, which Tony Wensleigh's bullet had shattered, had not been replaced, but the far side of the room, which was the part Charles was interested in, was clearly illuminated. He moved across through the bizarre juxtaposition of halberds and croquet mallets, fridges and thrones, wooden lampposts and polystyrene boulders.

He remembered Tony Wensleigh shuffling together a pile of breastplates when Charles had disturbed him. Had he been hiding something?

Charles started cautiously sifting through the armor. The breastplates were just the top of the pile. Beneath was an assortment of small props—cigar boxes, biscuit tins, ice buckets, jewel cases.

It didn't take him long to find what he was looking for.

They were inside a treasure chest. It was crudely painted, like something out of a pirate cartoon, and presumably only got an airing when the right pantomime came up. A fairly safe hiding-place, unlikely to be investigated from one year's end to the next.

They were papers, most of them with Antony Wensleigh's signature. Some meant nothing, but one or two Charles could identify.

There was a letter to the costume hire company, canceling the order for a Henry VIII ensemble.

There was a letter to the caretaker of the Drill Hall, confirming that the Regent Theatre wished to continue their booking.

There were checks to settle accounts with wigmakers and scenery builders, checks that never arrived, prompted reminders and lowered the theatre's public credibility.

There were charming letters to actors, which they never received and so added the Regent to the list of unhelpful theatres that didn't give a damn.

There was the whole history of the tarnishing of the public image of Antony Wensleigh and the theatre he so loved.

It must have been so simple. The props store was directly next to the administrative office. Tony Wensleigh would rush in early, before rehearsal, or late, after rehearsal, and scribble off a few letters. Donald Mason, in the office all day, would have leisure to select which letters could be mislaid to best effect and slip them into his secret cache whenever he wanted to. Then he had only to play on the Artistic Director's natural abstraction and vagueness to convince him of his omissions, meanwhile maintaining a whispering campaign about his colleague's inefficiency and perhaps worse.

But Tony had discovered what was going on and intended to reveal all to the Board at their Extraordinary Meeting.

First, though, he had confronted his enemy.

Charles decided to do the same. The discovery of the papers made him so angry that, whatever the risk, he had to satisfy the anger by another confrontation with Donald Mason.

He braced himself behind the front door of the props store.

Then he swung it open.

As he suspected, it opened straight into the administrative office.

But there was nobody there to confront. The room was empty.

Back in the props store, he looked again at the papers and realized their worthlessness. They confirmed Donald Mason's position as saboteur at the Regent, but he had already confessed to that. And that was the crime he would never be charged with.

With regard to murder, Charles still had nothing. Nothing but a strong conviction.

The note was not enough. He had been alone when he witnessed Donald pocketing it. Maybe forensic tests could prove it had been written a few weeks earlier than it was supposed to have been, but Charles didn't reckon much on his chances of persuading the police to get to the point of forensic tests.

No, he was stymied again. Lots of suspicion—no proof.

He felt furious. He looked at his watch. Still not half-past six. Frank Walby would probably still be in the pub. Back to Plan A for the evening. Get hideously smashed.

He stood there for one last moment in the props store.

Vividly his mind played back his last encounter with Tony Wensleigh.

The man had straightened the pile of breastplates and . . . something else. A string or something. He had tucked a string behind the grandfather clock.

Charles moved towards it. He couldn't see anything.

He shifted the clock around and light spilled into the spaces behind.

It wasn't a string. It was a wire.

A thin gray wire.

One end led down to the ventilation brick in the wall to the administrative office.

The other led into the back of the grandfather clock where the movement had once been, but where now nestled a portable cassette recorder.

The "Play" button and the "Record" button were both pressed down. But when Charles canceled them and tried to rewind, nothing happened. The batteries had been allowed to run down. No one had ever switched it off.

The man who switched it on had not lived to switch it off.

Metaphors, Charles reflected wryly, do also have literal meanings, as he recalled Martha Wensleigh's report of her husband's words on the evening of his death:

"He said he'd finally sorted it out. He said it had all been very confusing, but he was getting there. Soon he'd have it all taped and the pressure would be off."

* * *

Nella was still in the Green Room.

"Is there a cassette recorder anywhere in the building?" Charles asked, panting after his rush down the ladder.

She looked surprised. "Yes, there's one we sometimes use for playing in sound effects at outside rehearsals."

"Can I use it?"

The Green Room, he decided, was too public; the wrong person might walk in; so he took the recorder to the Number One dressing room, which had a door which locked.

"You come and listen, Nella. I want a witness."

"What is all this?"

But she was intrigued and followed him into the dressing room. He locked the door and put the cassette in the player. He switched on.

After the leader of the tape ran through, there was the sound of distant voices. "Do you recognize it?" asked Charles.

The pretty A.S.M. shook her head and craned forward to listen more acutely.

"You should recognize it. You've heard it enough times. It's the second Act of *The Message Is Murder*."

"Oh yes."

"As heard from the props store above the stage. Which is excellent, because it gives a time reference."

"But why is—"

"Ssh!"

Much closer than the voices, there was the sound of a door opening.

"Tony! What have you been doing in there?"

The voice was unmistakably that of Donald Mason.

"I've just been looking at some very interesting papers."

"Oh. Interesting to whom?"

"Interesting to the Board, certainly. As they will find out when they see them tomorrow evening."

"You still haven't said what you are referring to."

"I'm referring to all the letters of mine you've filched, as part of your campaign to get me out of this job."

"Ah." The monosyllable was uttered with the same infuriating coolness that Charles had suffered that afternoon.

"I don't know why you want to do it. I don't know whether it's me you're trying to destroy or the theatre, but I tell you, Donald, you won't succeed. Oh, you nearly got me. I nearly cracked. You did it very well, confusing me, making me unsure what I had done, what I hadn't done, getting me so that I didn't trust my own judgment. Yes, you nearly succeeded. But now the tables are turned. I am going to shoot you down in flames, Donald Mason. You'll never get another job in any theatre in the country after I've finished showing you up."

There was a short laugh from Mason. *"I'll survive that. I don't want another job in any theatre in the country. All right, you go to the Board, Tony. Tell your tales out of school, by all means. What do you think'll happen?"*

"You'll get the sack."

"Possibly. And what will happen to the Regent? Just another example of shaky management, internal bickering. So I took a few letters—I don't call that a major crime."

"And what do you call attempted murder?"

"I don't know what you're talking about." The bantering tone was abruptly gone from Mason's voice.

"I was checking something in the Wardrobe store the Wednesday before last. Between the matinée and the evening show. I saw you adjusting the rope for Gordon's hanging."

There was a grunt from the General Manager, as if he had been winded, and the Artistic Director went on. *"It never occurred to me what you were doing, or I would have gone and undone it. When Gordon was injured I still couldn't believe it. But now, Donald, I'm beginning to realize just how cold-blooded you are."*

"You don't plan to tell the Board about the hanging, surely?"

"Oh yes, I do. Though I think I might tell the police first."

There was a sudden sound of movement, then a scuffle, then Tony's voice, very tense, saying, *"Keep back."*

"Oh, a gun. How convenient." The tone of grim banter

was back. *"If it had to come to this, I had planned to use a syringe. But a gun with your fingerprints on it—even better."*

"Keep away, Donald! I'm not afraid to use this."

"Oh, but you are, Tony. Just let me get my gloves on and—"

"I will use it!"

"No. You haven't got it in you, Tony. It's not in your nature. You're just like everyone else—too full of the milk of human kindness to be properly efficient. Unlike ME!"

The last word was the cue for another assault. There was a tussle, then silence. When Tony's voice was heard again, it sounded very frail.

"No, Donald. You mustn't. You can't."

"Sorry. You've left me no alternative."

The bang was hideously loud, but unfortunately it was not loud enough to cover the liquid gurgle from Antony Wensleigh, nor the thump of what remained of his head hitting the desk.

Charles Paris looked up at Nella. Her eyes were full of tears.

This was no time for another amateur confrontation. This time he had strong enough evidence to take to the police.

Their initial skepticism vanished when they heard the tape. They accompanied Charles to the Regent Theatre and looked with interest as he showed them the cassette recorder and the cache of papers.

Later that evening, Donald Mason, rising property developer and the most efficient General Manager the Regent had ever had, was arrested at his flat and charged with the murder of Antony Wensleigh.

CHAPTER
TWENTY

"... BUT EVERYTHING WAS passed on and subtly distorted by Donald," said Nella, slightly breathlessly. She looked sensational, her color heightened by the wine and excitement. "I mean, do you remember that Symposium thing I had to go to with Tony... you know, the thing that meant Rick couldn't go to his radio recording... well, we all assumed that was just Tony being awkward, but it wasn't. Tony told me when we were there. Donald had accepted on his behalf, and Donald had nominated me to go with him."

"Poor old Tony. He just wouldn't stand up for himself. It took him a long time to accept that anyone would be capable of that kind of deceit."

"I know. Did you talk to his wife—widow, I mean?"

"Yes. I rang her before I came here."

"How did she sound?"

"Pretty terrible. But she was pleased when I told her. I mean, nothing's going to bring Tony back, but at least his name has been cleared from any suspicion."

"Yes."

There was a peaceful lull in their conversation. They were now the only customers in The Happy Friend Chinese Restaurant and Takeaway. Those people in Rugland Spa daring enough to eat Chinese food were certainly not daring enough to do so after eleven o'clock in the evening.

Charles sighed. "Thank God we got him. I thought he'd get away with it all. And what he was doing was so easy. The old 'Divide and rule' principle. And there can't be many places where it's easier to foster division than a provincial rep."

Nella smiled. She really was very pretty.

Charles tried not to look at her too lustfully as he continued, "So he carefully built up a general atmosphere of distrust, then staged the odd accident to keep the situation on the boil. Like poor old Gordon's hanging—bound to lead to more demands for an enquiry. And all the time he was just trying to put the theatre out of business. The sad thing is . . ." He took a rueful sip of wine. ". . . he's probably succeeded."

"You think the Regent'll close?"

"I can't see it avoiding it this time."

"But surely Schlenter Estates won't get the development?"

"Don't see why not."

"But once their connection with Donald is shown . . . I mean, he'll be a convicted murderer and . . ."

"I'll lay any money you care to mention that the connection could never be proved. People in a company like Schlenter are very canny—and particularly when they've got Carker Glyde behind them. No, if there ever were an investigation, it would be proved that Donald Mason was acting off his own bat."

"They'd just drop him like that?"

"You bet. They'd show the same qualities of loyalty as he did."

Nella looked pensive. She was young, perhaps she still nursed some illusions about how the commercial world worked.

"Do you fancy a sweet, Nella?"

"Wonder what he's got."

"Mr. Pang!"

"Yes, sir."

"What have you got in the way of Ice Creams (Various)?"

"Today, sir," Mr. Pang announced with a huge conspiratorial grin, "we have Vanilla."

Through their laughter Charles and Nella agreed that they'd both have one. As the giggles subsided, Charles said thoughtfully, "One thing I still haven't worked out . . ."

"What's that?"

"Going back to the second night of *The Message Is Murder* . . . the night when I got so disgracefully pissed . . ."

"I remember."

"Well, somebody tried to stab me through the flat at the back of the cupboard and I never—"

He looked at Nella. She was blushing deeply.

"You?"

She nodded. "I've felt awful about it ever since."

"Well . . . What had I done?"

"It wasn't aimed at you, you fool."

"Then who did you think was in there?"

"No, I knew you were in there. Listen, if you remember, I was on the book that night, actually stage-managing the show, which meant I had to sit at the desk and couldn't move about much. And someone took advantage of that . . ."

"Leslie Blatt?"

"Got it in one. He kept sneaking up behind me and making the most disgusting suggestions. And then touching me up and . . . ugh. Eventually I got so furious, I just jumped up and chased him with the sword. I really wanted to kill him, I lunged at him . . ."

"And he moved out of the way."

She nodded shamefacedly. "Yes. I felt terrible when I realized what I'd done. I thought I'd killed you for sure."

Charles grinned. "Well, you didn't."

"No. Thank God."

"Must be pretty ghastly," he said casually, "for a young girl, being touched up by older men."

She turned her astonishingly beautiful face to him and gave a little shy grin. "Depends on the older man."

Charles Paris looked at her hand lying on the table. Nice hand—small, but strong. No rings, nails a bit grubby from making props all day.

His hand moved forward and hovered over hers . . .

*   *   *

Charles's prognostication for the future of the theatre proved
too pessimistic. The new offer from Schlenter Estates had its
predictable effect in the Council Chamber, and it seemed
that the Regent would finally be demolished as part of the
Maugham Cross redevelopment scheme.

But local support came from an unlikely source. Mrs.
Feller, seeing there was a cause to champion, marshalled her
Hats and, after a well-orchestrated sequence of banner-
waving demonstrations and letters in the *Rugland Spa Ga-
zette & Observer* (backed up by fighting leaders from Frank
Walby), the Council decision was rescinded. Councilor
Davenport was furious, and Councilor Inchbald was delighted.

The Arts Council, too, decided to give the theatre another
chance. Given the fact that there would be a new Artistic
Director and General Manager, the Regent got its grant.
And the Council agreed to match it.

Herbie Inchbald remained as Chairman of the The-ettah
Board. But Lord Kitestone also remained as the Regent's
patron; and the Maugham Cross area got increasingly run
down; one day it would have to be developed. So the
theatre's ultimate future remained uncertain.

But, in the manner of provincial theatres, from crisis to
crisis, the Regent continued to totter on.

Incidentally, those who care about that sort of thing would
feel cheated not to be informed that the suicide of Miss
Laycock-Manderley in Act Three of *The Message Is Murder*
was a blind. She Did It.

SIMON BRETT is the author of thirteen Charles Paris mysteries as well as a collection of short stories and four other novels. A scriptwriter and radio and television producer, he is a former president of the British Crime Writers' Association. He lives in England.